SEATTLE
WALDORF
SCHOOL

2728 NE 100th Street
Seattle, WA 98125

The Falconer

The Falconer

by

Christopher Sblendorio

AWSNA

Printed with support from the Waldorf Curriculum Fund

Published by:
The Association of Waldorf Schools
of North America
Publications Office
65–2 Fern Hill Road
Ghent, NY 12075

Title: *The Falconer*
Author: Christopher Sblendorio
Editor: David Mitchell
Illustrator: Amy Inglis
Proofreader: Ann Erwin
Cover: David Mitchell
© 2010 by AWSNA
ISBN # 978-1-888365-94-8

Printed by McNaughton & Gunn
Saline, MI 48176 USA
February 2010

Table of Contents

Acknowledgments 8

Introduction 9

Pronunciation Guide 11

Maps: The Mediterranean Area............................... 12
         The Holy Roman Empire 13
         The Kingdom of Sicily 14

Prologue – Remembering.. 15

Chapter 1 – A Wondrous Birth 17

Federico is born in a town square. He becomes
an orphan and a ward of the Church.

Chapter 2 – A Wild Child.. 23

Federico has a great heritage. Although he has
good teachers, he learns much on the streets
of Palermo.

Chapter 3 – A Bridling with a Bride 29

At fifteen years old Federico marries Constance
of Aragon.

Chapter 4 — Adventures in the North:
From a King to an Emperor 35

Frederick makes a long, dangerous journey to
Germany to become the Holy Roman Emperor.
He meets the Pope.

Chapter 5 — Interests in the South: Of Birds and Castles 44

Frederick writes his famous book on ornithology
and builds a unique castle.

Chapter 6 — The Cavalcade and the Cafun 54

Frederick's cavalcade is seen through the eyes
of peasants.

Chapter 7 — A Meeting with a Saint 61

Frederick meets Francis of Assisi and tests his
piety.

Chapter 8 — A Meeting with the Wise Men 65

Frederick shares his interests with the greatest
scholars of the time.

Chapter 9 — Problems with the Popes 70

The Popes see Frederick as an evil man.

Chapter 10 — Many Wives and Many Children 74

Frederick's personal life is revealed through his
wives and children.

Chapter 11 – Friends and Enemies................................. 80

> The Pope incites the northern Italian cities to
> rebel and excommunicates Frederick.

Chapter 12 – A Great Loss... 84

> Frederick loses an important battle and one of
> his sons. A prophecy is fulfilled at his death.

Chapter 13 – The Vendetta... 91

> The Pope has Frederick's family killed.

Chapter 14 – The Future.. 97

> Frederick was seen as both good and bad.
> He pointed to the future.

Notes..102

Further Reading...104

Acknowledgments

Thanks go to my friends and family in Italy who shared with me their homes, culture, historical landmarks, and interest in my enthusiasm for discovering all I could about Frederick.

Thanks go to my dear class of 2004 who, when they were in 6th grade, took on the huge task of performing the play that I wrote for them, *The Falconer*. They were marvelous, especially Frederick—Amy Inglis, a most upright and noble character.

Great thanks go to my dear friend and encourager, Billie Chernicoff, who read my manuscript and whittled away my verbosity, making this story easier to read.

Many, many thanks go to my long time friend, Penelope Lord, who watched all the changes with an eagle's eye. Besides being a good advisor, she put my pencilled-on-legal-paper manuscript into type, a marvelous feat. She also loves Frederick as much as I do.

Of course the sweetest thanks go to my beloved Barbara, my best friend and wife, who listened to hours and hours of my recounting Frederick's life and followed me all over Italy in pursuit of him.

Introduction

I first came across Federico II ten years ago when I was reading H.M. Morton's *A Traveler in Southern Italy*. Morton's description of Frederick traveling across his kingdom with his cavalcade, so like a circus with its animals and performers, delighted me. His description of Frederick's book on falconry intrigued me. When I saw an example of a page from this book, I was amazed. It looked like a page from one of my students' lesson-journals. It was hand-written with beautiful penmanship. It had illustrated borders and hand-drawn colored pictures of birds and people. I was convinced that this was no ordinary king or emperor. Seeing a picture of his Castel Del Monte made me want to see the real castle. I did so when I went to Italy on my sabbatical to visit my many relatives in the southern region of Puglia, the heel of the Italian boot.

That first visit was an adventure. In those days people could still drive up to the castle, but it didn't feel right to me to arrive in a car, so I left my car at the bottom of the hill below the castle and walked up to it through a pine forest. What an uplifting experience it was to come out of the trees and see the castle, its pale, luminous geometry crowning the hilltop. After walking through the rooms of the castle, I stood in the inner octagonal courtyard. I took out my button accordion and played for the castle. In that space the little accordion sounded like a gigantic pipe organ, the sound of it reverberating off the walls.

Later, I met some people from the city next to the village where my relatives live. They were also teachers and musicians, and had a band that played folk music. I visited them often and played music with them. Their band played the soundtrack for a movie called *Io Non Ho La Testa (I Don't Have a Head)*, which is about Federico II at Castel Del Monte.

Each succeeding summer when I visited my friends and family in southern Italy, I discovered another of Federico's castles. I began to read everything I could find about him. The more I learned about him, the more I learned that there would always be more to learn. I told my students about his life when they were studying the Middle Ages in sixth grade. I wrote a play for them called *The Falconer*, which they enjoyed working on and performed brilliantly.

In the summer following the performance of *The Falconer*, I went to Sicily. I thought then that my fascination with Federico II had reached a finale. In Palermo I visited the various Norman-Arabic palaces and churches. I went to the Cathedral Santa Maria Assunta to visit Federico's tomb. After buying a bouquet of red roses, I went in and stood before his tomb. Placing the roses in a vase in front of the tomb, I put my hand on his tomb and said, "There, it is done."

But it was not done. I continued to find his life interesting. I read more, learned more, visited more places where he had dwelt. I came to realize that while the play my students had performed had brought Federico II to their schoolmates, parents, and friends, his life and adventures were great enough to be brought to the attention of more people, especially to young students interested in the Middle Ages. This book is the result of that realization.

Was Federico a good man or a bad man? Both, I think, but more than that, he was a great man. My friends in northern Italy say he was a bad emperor. My friends in southern Italy say he was a good king. It is amazing that today, over seven hundred years after his death, the Italians continue to have strong opinions about him. In southern Italy the people talk about him as if he were alive just yesterday. Travelers from Germany to southern Italy still visit the places he made famous. They still have an interest in the Holy Roman Emperor from Sicily.

When Frederick II is mentioned, most people think of Frederick the Great, King of Prussia, who lived during the eighteenth century (1712–1786). But Federico II of Hohenstaufen was a medieval emperor who was not just great but who was called the "Wonder of the World."

Pronunciation Guide

Some of the names of the characters in this book are not common in English and may present a challenge to the reader.

In Italian each vowel is sounded separately and pronounced quickly.

An *a* always sounds like *ah*, *e* like *ay* or *eh*, *i* like *ee*, *o* like *oh* or *aw*, *u* like *oo*.

Before *e* or *i*, a *g* sounds like the *g* in *gem*. Before other vowels, *g* sounds like the *g* in *go*.

C and *ch* are opposite in Italian and English. In Italian, when you read a *c*, pronounce it as a *ch*, and pronounce a *ch* as an English *c*. For example, *chi* would be pronounced *key*, and *che* would be pronounced *kay*. But, *ce* would be *chay*, and *ci* would be *chee*. Also, *ca* would be *kah*. *Co* and *cu* get open vowels, *coh* and *coo*.

If you remember to keep the vowels open, as in singing, you will get the right spirit of the language. Also stress the next-to-last syllable for the correct accent.

Dialect words turn up in the sixth chapter. A *cafone* means country bumpkin. In southern Italian dialect, it comes out *cafun*, "cah-foon." Many of the dialect words are funny and should be enjoyed for the fun of it. For example, *uaglio*, meaning a guy, is pronounced "wahl-yo," and *uè*, meaning hey!, is pronounced "oo-ay" and sounds like "way."

I have used Italian words and phrases in the dialogues and usually follow them with their equivalent in English, so you should understand the Italian and not lose the meaning but enjoy the music of the language.

Maps

The Mediterranean Area

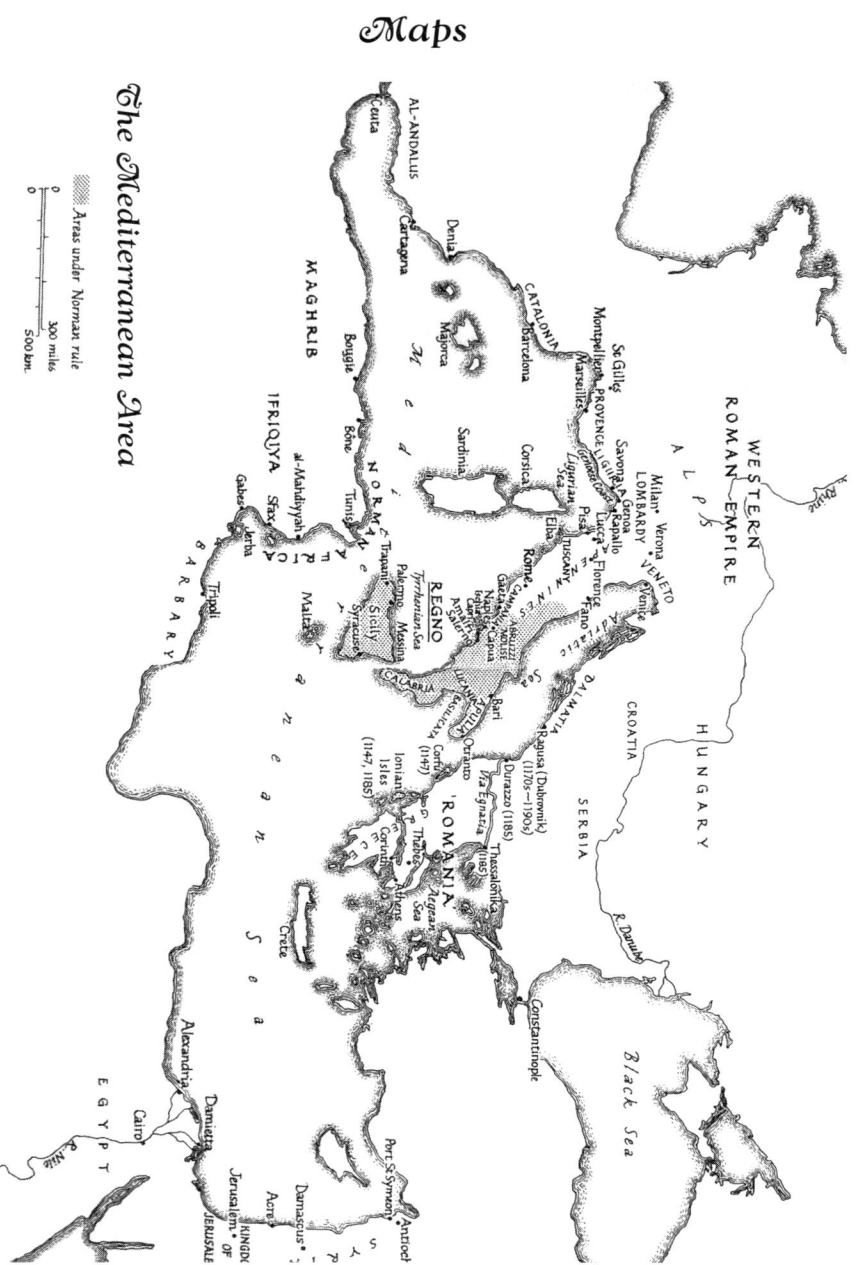

The Holy Roman Empire
during the time of Federico II

The
Kingdom of Sicily

Prologue

Remembering

"*Vola, cara mia!* Fly, my lovely! Soar, my sweet. If only I could fly like you. Swift, and directly to my goal. But, alas ..."

The emperor's falcon flew from his wrist and soared from the castle turret over the expansive plain. The emperor's eyes watched the majestic flight of one of his beautiful birds. The falcon's sharp eyes searched the country for prey. As the bird searched for food, the emperor searched for answers to the many problems that plagued his kingdom. Finally, the emperor's musing was interrupted by the entrance of his chief counselor and good friend, Piero Della Vigna.

"Federico, *mi dispiace.* I am sorry to disturb you again," he said, bowing as he spoke.

"Piero, *caro amico*, my dearest friend, if I must be disturbed, it is good to be disturbed by you. What is it?" Federico responded warmly.

Piero handed the emperor a letter and said, "I bring you greetings from your comrade and ally, Louis."

Federico was pleased and asked, "The King of France? An answer to my letter?"

"No," was the answer Piero gave.

The emperor's disappointment was obvious. "No? Alas, what is it?"

"Greetings for your birthday. *Buon compleanno.*"

"But my birthday was long ago."

Piero smiled and handed the heavily ornamented letter to Federico. "The couriers ride horses over mountains, rivers, valleys, long distances, and they don't have wings as your dear birds do. It takes time for letters to travel. Luckily, our thoughts don't take so long."

Federico took the letter, weighed it in his hands, turned it over and over, and began to think. Aloud he said, almost to himself, "My birthday, 52 years ago, 1194, December 26, the day after Christmas. So long ago ..."

Chapter 1

A Wondrous Birth

If we could travel back in time to that Christmas season, we would find ourselves in Italy, in a small town near the city of Ancona, on the east coast, about midway along the peninsula. It was the rainy season; the weather would have been cold and damp, a cold that seeps into your bones, that you can't escape.

Empress Constance had traveled all the way to Germany from sunny Sicily to marry the Emperor Henry VI. After the wedding, Henry hurried ahead of her to establish himself as the ruler of southern Italy, as well as the Holy Roman Empire in Germany. The Empress followed him later, traveling slowly with her retinue of courtiers, ladies-in-waiting to attend to her needs, and soldiers to guard her. She was carrying a precious treasure with her, her soon-to-be-born child, the future emperor. It had been a long, arduous journey over the high mountains of the Alps.

"I can go no further," said the fatigued Empress.

"Yes, my Lady Constance, let us stop," said her maid. "You seem exhausted."

"Where are we now? What town is this?" asked the weary traveler.

"This is Jesi, your grace."

"Jesi?"

"It was named after our Lord Jesus."

"Then here shall my child be born. My husband Emperor Henry waits for me in Sicilia, but he will have to wait longer. I can go no further. My child cannot wait any longer. He longs to see the light of day."

Her waiting maid said, "We will find lodgings for your escort of knights, and the finest house in this town for you."

"No! Send the knights to gather all the bishops of all the cities within the three nearest provinces and have them brought here immediately to be my witnesses."

"My lady? But ..."

"I am forty-one years old and with child. Without many reliable, trustworthy and honorable witnesses, Henry's enemies will claim that my child is not the true heir to the thrones of Italy and Germany. Germany is his through Henry, and Italy through me."

"My Lady Constance, let us find appropriate lodgings!"

"No. I want a large tent set up in this very piazza."

"In this town square?!" the shocked serving maid asked.

"Yes, right here," the Empress replied.

"On these streets?"

"Here is where my child will be born, in public, with the Church Fathers as my witnesses."

When the bishops arrived days later, they waited for the imminent birth. They were lodged in the finest houses that the town had to offer. The town was filled with their retinues, and the townsfolk were constantly busy keeping them fed and entertained.

Christmas came and was celebrated by the bishops in grand fashion. Winding through the narrow streets, they led the procession to the Church of Saint Nicolo. Dressed in their finest vestments, they glittered with gold thread. Behind them followed an endless stream of monks from the many surrounding monasteries. Once in the church they sang the High Mass of the feast day, which lasted hours, leaving the air thick with the smoke of frankincense. Their midday dinner was served in the refectory of the largest monastery and lasted until late in the evening.

On the following day the bishops were summoned to the birth of Constance's child. There in the tent in the piazza she gave birth and declared, "This is my child, bear me witness! This is my child, a boy. He shall carry his grandfathers' names, Emperor Frederick Barbarossa I and King Roger II of Sicily. He is my son, Frederick Roger. I, Constance of Hauteville, heir to Norman Sicily, declare this child my son, and his father is Henry of Hohenstaufen. This is our son. Be my witnesses!"

Then she breathed a sigh of relief, and said to her waiting maids, "I would like to name him Constantine after myself. But I will call him Federico."

With his brows knitted, Frederick said, "I did not see my mother again for three years. She left me in Jesi with the Duchess of Spoleto who lovingly cared for me during my infancy.

"My father demanded that she join him immediately in the city of Bari to be crowned king and queen of Sicily on Easter Sunday. My cousin, William II, the Good, was the last Norman king on the throne of Sicily, and he willed it to my mother, his aunt. My other cousin, Tancred, took the throne because my mother wasn't married and was living in a convent. But when my father married her, he demanded the crown and throne from Tancred. Oh, these royal families are so complicated!"

Piero added, "Your father was absolutely brutal to the people who considered Tancred the rightful king. Your mother was horrified by his cruelty and did what she could to stop him. There was great tension between them as a result."

"How could she have left her infant son behind in Jesi?" wondered Frederick. "And I never knew my father. You know, Piero, he died when I was only three years old. After his death, my mother sent some trusted noblemen from Puglia to go north to fetch me from the Duchess of Spoleto. I didn't understand what was happening when I was taken away from her. She was more of a mother to me than my own mother, whom I didn't even know then. But I remember my mother's tears when we first met and she told me of my father's death. She said later that she cried for my loss of a father more than for her loss of a husband."

Piero reflected on what Federico had said and added, "Your mother, Empress Constance, died soon after your father."

"Yes," answered the emperor, with a faraway look in his eyes. "I was four years old then, but I still remember what she said to me. She called me to her side as she lay on her deathbed: " 'Federico, *caro mio. Vieni, vieni qua, figlio mio.* Come here, my son. *Figlio mio*, never forget that you are Italian. This is your country, your people. Your father was a German emperor, and I am the daughter of a Norman king. But you, you are Italian. You were born and raised in Italy, and you must keep Italy dear in your heart, dear Federico. When I am gone I will leave you in the safekeeping of the Pope of Rome, Innocent III.'"

The Pope received the news of Constance's death at a time when he was too busy to give it much notice. He was fighting a crusade, not against the Moslems in the Holy Land, but against the people of southern France, the people of Provence called Cathars. These people were Christians who objected to the wealth and power of the Roman Catholic Church. When he had a moment to give the news of Constance's death some thought, Innocent III accepted the responsibility of caring for the orphaned heir to the thrones of Italy and Germany. After all, the Pope's lands, the Papal States, were wedged between the Kingdom of Southern Italy and the Holy Roman Empire to the north. Both realms were lands that Frederick would one day rule. But until then, this small boy would need protection, and Pope Innocent III was one of the most powerful men in Europe. He said to the cardinals who waited on him, "The Empress is dead. Her son Frederick is now a ward of the Holy Mother Church. I am his Papal Father, and we must keep Sicily and southern Italy." After a pause, he added, "We must keep them safe for him, of course."

Fig 1. The prone child and teachers

Chapter 2

A Wild Child

In the city of Palermo, life for Federico was very different from what was expected for the heir to the throne of Sicily. Palermo was the capital city of Sicily and southern Italy. It was one of the wealthiest cities in Europe at that time, as well as a great cultural center, rich in art. After the fall of the ancient Roman Empire, the barbarian tribes of the north took control of Sicily. They were pushed out by the Byzantine Greeks, who were then conquered by the Arabs. These Moslems ruled for three hundred years. They were tolerant of their Christian and Jewish subjects. It was a cosmopolitan realm with Sicilian, Greek, Hebrew, and Arabic people living and working together.

After they lost Sicily to the Arabs, the Byzantine Greeks still held southern Italy. These two groups fought each other again and again. The Arabs attacked southern Italy. The Byzantines attacked Sicily. Then a third group arrived, the Lombards, a Germanic people who had control of northern Italy. They too tried to take southern Italy from the Byzantines. Then the Normans came from France to fight in the Crusades, in the Holy Lands of the Middle East. When these red-haired warriors from the cold north passed through sunny southern Italy, they were asked by the Lombards to help push out the Byzantine

Greeks. The Normans willingly fought the Greeks and won. Then they turned on their Lombard allies, defeated them, and took control of all of southern Italy. The Normans then turned their attention to the island of Sicily. They fought the Arabs, and although they were greatly outnumbered, they gained Sicily, the jewel of the Mediterranean. The Kingdom of Sicily was made up of both the island of Sicily and all the lands south of Rome.

By Christmas Day 1130, Roger II d'Hauteville, Federico's Norman grandfather, was crowned King of Sicily, with the Pope's blessing, in the cathedral of Palermo. The cathedral, which formerly had been a mosque, was packed with ambassadors, legates, and ministers from all over the known world.

Chronicles of the times report that the world had never seen such splendor as there was during the reign of King Roger II d'Hauteville. There were marvelous pleasure gardens with fountains and baths with running water, a luxury virtually unknown in the rest of medieval Europe. The seaport was full of merchants and ships from all over the Mediterranean. Luxurious silks and cottons were produced. Agriculture thrived, yielding a bounty of fruits and grains. The palaces, like the Ziza and the Cuba, and the cathedrals and chapels were glorious with mosaics, the works of both Christian and Moslem craftsmen. In the streets of Palermo, voices could be heard speaking the many different languages of the people of Sicily: Latin and Greek, Hebrew and Arabic, French and German, and, of course, Sicilian.

King Roger kept most of the Arab administration intact, seeing that it functioned well in governing the country. The court doctors and poets were Arabs as well. He adopted the dress and many of the customs of his new subjects. He established a splendid kingdom that his daughter Constance would inherit and pass on to her son.

The walls of the Cathedral in Montreale near Palermo were adorned with intricate mosaics and gold. An important one showed Roger being crowned by God, not by the Pope, making it clear that Roger believed his rulership was bestowed on him by the highest source. He had his throne in the cathedral made three steps higher than the bishop's throne, again to display his belief that the king was more important than the religious leader, a conviction that Frederick would inherit.

But the Palermo in which Federico was growing up was a different world than that of his grandfather's. After his mother's death, he was supposed to be under the care of the Pope, but the Pope was in Rome, and Federico received little attention from him or from his father's German courtiers, who were struggling to gain power in Sicily. Because of their neglect, Federico's care fell to his tutors, who often had to ask for food and clothing on his behalf.

When he could, Federico would roam the streets of Palermo, but when he was with his tutors, they taught him many subjects to prepare him to be a true king. He would ask his teachers: "*Perchè?!* Why?! Why must I learn Latin?"

His Greek teacher would answer, "You must also learn Greek."

"But why?" Federico groaned. His Arabic teacher was listening intently, but said nothing. His Latin teacher answered him, "Latin is spoken by all learned men. It is the universal language."

"Greek!" said his Greek teacher. "The ancient Greeks were the most learned people because they spoke the language of philosophy."

"But now it is the Latin of the Church that is most important," said the Latin teacher.

"Which church? Your church?" asked the Greek teacher.

"The most Holy and Roman Catholic Church," answered the Latin teacher.

"But the Gospels were first written in Greek," responded the Greek teacher.

"*Ma, perchè?*" asked Federico again. "But why?"

"Why what?" cried both teachers as the Arabic teacher continued to listen.

"Why must I learn Greek or Latin? I speak Italian perfectly."

"Perfectly? You speak Italian like a Sicilian street urchin."

"Well, I have also learned to speak my father's German."

"Hardly!"

"And my mother's French!"

"Not much better."

Now the Arabic teacher called out, "Allah be praised! He also speaks Arabic like the many Saracen people of Sicily."

"He must also learn to use a sword," said the Greek teacher, to which the Latin teacher replied: "And how to hunt with birds—*de arte venandi cum avibus.*"

The Arabic teacher added, "And he must also learn to ride an Arabian stallion like a master."

As they all began arguing all over again, Federico sneaked away to adventures in Palermo. "Latin! Greek! Allah be praised!" The tutors shouted at each other, while Federico ran off yelling, "I'm free!"

In the streets, Federico did not appear kingly. He looked like any boy of modest means. The other boys, whose parents were merchants and fishermen, called him Rico for short.

"*Uè uaglio,* Rico! *Come stai?!* Hey man, Rico! How are you?"

The Greek merchants would greet him, his face being a familiar one in their quarters. "*Kali spera,* Federico. Good evening."

The Arab merchants also knew him well. "Allah be praised," was their greeting.

"May Allah grant all your wishes," was his response.

"Allah have mercy on that poor orphan," they said amongst themselves.

"*Bon jour, mon ami.* Good day, my friend," called the French courtiers on their way to the pleasure gardens on the edge of the city.

"*Bon jour. Ça va?* Good day. How's it going?" Federico replied.

"*Bien, merci.* Well, thanks. *Et vous?* And you?" answered one of the gentlemen.

"*Ça va, va bien, merci,*" Federico called back, as he approached one of the city gateways where two soldiers from the German guards stood.

"*Du!* You!" called out one of the men.

"*Wie geht es Ihnen?*" said Federico in his best German.

"*Was sagen Sie?* What do you say?" asked the soldier.

"*Wenn Fliegen hinter Fliegen fliegen, Fliegen fliegen Fliegen nach.* When flies fly behind flies, flies fly after flies," said Federico.

"*Ja, ja, das stimmt!* Yes, yes, that's right!" laughed the soldiers at Federico's clever wit.

He showed his clever hands by snatching an orange from the fruit stand of a big fat merchant with a great huge mustache. The sharp-eyed fruit vendor caught Federico by the wrist, and, knowing who he was, yelled, "*Ma perchè?* But why?"

"*Perchè no?* Why not?"

"*Perchè*, because you are the king. Why do you steal?"

"*Ho fame!*" the boy cried. "I'm famished!"

"But you are the king. How can you be hungry? Why should a king have to steal food?"

"I'm not king yet!"

"But you are! Or will be soon enough. To us you are our king already."

"*Senti.* Listen. Then I am the king. *Vero?* Right?"

"*Vero*," answered the patient merchant.

"Then you are my subject. *Vero?*"

"*Certo.* Certainly," answered the less patient merchant.

"As king, the land of this country belongs to me."

"*Si*, yes," replied the curious merchant.

"And on my land grows this fruit."

"*Aspett'.* Wait," the disbelieving merchant said slowly.

"So I am only taking what belongs to me."

"*Aspett'*," said the suspicious merchant.

"And so you should pay me for this fruit that I took!" Federico concluded triumphantly.

"*Mannaggia!* Darn!" exclaimed the defeated merchant.

"And eat," said Federico, taking a big bite into the orange peel and tearing it open as he ran off through the crowd that had gathered to witness this amusing encounter.

"*Uè!* Hey!" laughed the merchant, the bystanders laughing with him. "*Statta bbuon.* Be good," he called after Federico. And to himself he said, "*Dio mio!* My God!" and slapped the palm of his hand against his forehead. That really made the crowd laugh. An orange was a small fee to pay for such a good laugh. "The price of these oranges has just doubled," called out the jolly merchant, "because they belong to the king, the future King Federico!"

The future king stopped in a piazza and joined a group of *giovanotti*, young people, who were beginning to dance a *tarantella.* The players beat out the rhythm on the big tambourines as they sang. The dancers stepped and twirled with Federico in their midst. Suddenly he heard his name called, "Federico!" His teachers had found him at last. The music stopped and the dancers stood around him.

"I am twelve years old. Being king means freedom," Federico fumed.

"Freedom means responsibility," his teachers answered—in Latin, Greek, and Arabic all at the same time.

"But also," Federico called out in frustration as he stormed off to the royal palace, "freedom from guardians, freedom from regents, and freedom from teachers!"

Chapter 3

A Bridling with a Bride

In Rome Pope Innocent III was also thinking about Federico's freedom, but his thoughts were very different from those of the young king. Innocent knew that if he was to maintain and increase his control of the political life of Europe, he would need to control the future king of southern Italy and emperor of the Holy Roman Empire, especially as Federico grew older. So Innocent needed to learn more about him, and he discussed the boy with his cardinals. He asked them detailed questions about his character and temperament.

"This ward of the Holy Mother Church, this orphan boy, how old is he now?"

"Fourteen, Your Grace, but he behaves like a licentious man of thirty," answered one cardinal.

"He educates himself on the streets of Palermo and ignores the excellent teachers assigned to him," added another.

The first cardinal continued, "Federico already knows the ways of grown men."

"And women!" added the second cardinal. "Why, he chases the young women ... and older women!"

"Does he respect his teachers?" the Pope wanted to know.

"Well, yes, but he doesn't really listen to them. He is constantly questioning them. Why this and why that and what proof is there? Chatter, chatter, chatter!"

The second cardinal added, "And his assignments are always late, late, late, if done at all."

"How is he formed?" asked the Pope, "and of what humor is he?"

"He is short of stature, like his mother," said the first cardinal, adding, "weak and sickly."

The second cardinal continued, "He wouldn't fetch much money on the African slave market. Not very handsome."

At that moment, the Archbishop Berardo of Palermo, a great supporter and friend of Federico's, came to the door. He had just arrived from Sicily having been summoned by the Pope to report to him. He stopped in the doorway, listening to what was being said before crossing the large room to kneel before the throne and kiss the ring on the Pope's hand. Berardo said, "But he is strong, and daily exercises both mind and body. He is good with bow and arrow, a fine swordsman, an excellent horseman. He is spirited—with red hair like his Norman ancestors. The people call him *Il Stupor Mundi*, the Wonder of the World, Amazing Frederick, and I, as the Archbishop of Palermo, I give him my blessing."

The Pope thought about these two different views of Federico and surprised his cardinals with his response. "His abundance of energy needs to be tempered if he cannot be controlled. He needs a wife, an older woman. The King of Hungary's widow has been returned to her parents in Aragon, Spain. She is ten years his elder and bears his mother's name, Constance. It will be a marriage blessed by our special favor."

Archbishop Berardo was assigned the task of informing Constance of Aragon that Pope Innocent III wished her to marry Frederick of Sicily. He put it this way for her: "*You are entering a magnificent marriage. Frederick is distinguished by the majesty of his virtues as well as his inheritance of a kingdom rich and noble among the kingdoms of* the world—southern Italy—a favored port, Palermo, the meeting place of all the lands surrounding the Mediterranean Sea—Sicily, the navel of the world."

Constance accepted the marriage arrangement gracefully. She traveled to Palermo with a grand retinue of five hundred knights. They arrived in the heat of the summer of 1209. The seaport was crowded with ships from all over the Mediterranean. As the bride's ships sailed into the harbor, the bells of all the churches began to ring. When Constance disembarked, she was radiantly dressed, and so was Palermo. The golden domes on the hundreds of Arab mosques, the colorful mosaics of the Greek Byzantine churches, the Jewish synagogues with their swirling designs, the great cathedral Santa Maria Assunta, the palaces surrounded by orange and lemon trees in flower, their fragrance wafting through the air, all these greeted Constance. The surrounding golden mountains were covered with silvery olive trees glistening as they waved in the breeze. The streets were crowded with masses of people, all curious and hoping to catch a glimpse of the new queen. She was slender, graceful, and young, although ten years older than Frederick. The blue of her brocade gown and the clear blue of her eyes were set off by her yellow-blond hair. From the crowds watching her ride through the streets came the sound of the sea, a sea of whispering people admiring the queen's majesty.

But Federico would not meet his bride until the day before they were to be married, according to custom. He was not happy about how his future bride was being presented to him. As he dressed in his best to meet her, he complained bitterly to his tutors and servants and Archbishop Berardo. "But I am not yet fifteen. I don't want to get married! She is twenty-five years old! And a widow! Not even a virgin! I am the king. I will decide ..." At that moment the door opened for the entrance of Constance and her waiting maids. "... to marry ... this marvelous beauty ... with blue eyes ... like mine ... she is a revelation." To Constance he said, *"Buenos dias, mia cara amiga."*

She laughed like a peal of bells. "He speaks my language," she said.

Fig 2. Frederick greeting Constance

Federico confided to the Archbishop, "She is like a dream, like a wish come true, someone I longed for, the fulfillment of a deep desire."

Constance said to the Archbishop, "I am well pleased, my lord," as she took Federico's hand.

"No one has taken my hand since my mother's death, when I was four years old. I, too, am well pleased, my lord Archbishop," said Federico.

"So long ago," said Frederick to Piero della Vigna. "That was forty long years ago."

"How we have all changed since then," said Archbishop Berardo as he entered the room to join Frederick and Piero. He continued, "Constance liked your uprightness. Attracted by the light hair that curled about your neck, she found you handsome. She was amazed at your knowledge of so many things, your interest in everything."

"Yes," responded Frederick, "we talked for hours on end. She told me sad stories of Pope Innocent III's crusade against the people of her homeland, the Cathar heretics, and of how the king of France and his nobles destroyed the beautiful country of Provence."

"She found you a paragon of a husband," added Piero, "but was perplexed by your changing moods."

"She was calm and quiet by nature, yet independent and self-confident," said Frederick, to which the Archbishop replied, "She found you docile as a lamb one moment and immovable as a mountain the next. Your gentleness and humor would change suddenly into bold defiance, and your eyes would flash fire. A playful innocent child one minute and a cynical old man the next, mistrusting of others."

"Constance told me about the wonders of the courts of Aragon and Provence," said Frederick, "the knights and their code of chivalry, the poets, the troubadours and song contests, the tournaments in honor of fair ladies, the music and musical instruments."

The Archbishop continued, "Many of those troubadours and so-called heretics came to your court and found a new and safe home here. They were enriched by the Greek, Arab, Jewish, French and Italian courtiers, and added their art and knowledge to your court. That influenced you and you changed because of her."

"How I loved and respected her," said Frederick. "How I missed her when she died so young. I put my crown in her tomb as a token of my love."

Fig 3. Constance's crown

Chapter 4

Adventures in the North: From a King to an Emperor

Two short years after Frederick and Constance were married, Frederick, now seventeen years of age, became a father. He named his son Henry, after his own father. But an even greater adventure than fatherhood lay in the future path of the young king.

When his father, Emperor Henry VI, died shortly after Frederick's birth, the German princes elected Otto of Saxony to be the Holy Roman Emperor. Pope Innocent III confirmed the election and placed the imperial crown on Otto's head, having gained his agreement to leave southern Italy alone. But Otto had other ideas, and, shortly after Frederick and Constance were married, in spite of his oath not to invade Frederick's lands, he marched his armies south. He reached Calabria, the toe of Italy, and was ready to cross the Straits of Messina to Sicily. His plan was to march to Palermo and take this gem of the Mediterranean away from Frederick, whose forces were weak compared to Otto's army. Frederick and Constance were preparing to escape by ship when suddenly everything changed. The Pope excommunicated Otto for breaking his promise, expelled him from the Holy Mother Church, clearing the way for the German princes to drop their oaths of allegiance to Otto. So Otto turned his armies northward to regain his crown by force and contest the action of the princes who now wanted to elect Frederick emperor.

Frederick decided that his destiny was to go north to receive the crown from the princes and then travel to Rome to gain the Pope's confirmation and blessing. It was difficult for Constance to let her husband leave her and their newborn son. Germany was far away, and Frederick's journey would be perilous. But if he succeeded, he would be the Holy Roman Emperor. "It is time that I take the crown that rightly belongs to me," Frederick told his dear wife. "I will be Holy Roman Emperor, like my father and grandfather before me."

Constance, looking him deeply in the eyes, took both his hands and said, "But you have to travel all the way to Germany to have the princes and nobles elect you. Must you go? Is not Italy kingdom enough for you? The way is dangerous. There are those in both Italy and Germany who do not want you crowned emperor."

"My love, this is something I must do. I will send for you when I have safely arrived, am crowned, and have been recognized as emperor and king. I promise with all my heart." He took her hands and placed them on his heart. She pulled him to her and hugged him hard.

"Farewell, my dear one," he said.

"Farewell, my love."

Frederick left without hesitation, ready to start his long, adventurous journey. He was now just eighteen years old. His friends and courtiers did not support his plan to travel to Germany to become emperor, so he did not demand that they accompany him. Instead, he left Palermo by ship with only a few attendants and no armed guards.

The Archbishop Berardo suggested that he go by way of Rome to receive the Pope's blessing on his endeavor. Frederick agreed to this, and the Archbishop traveled with him.

Otto of Saxony tried his best to prevent Frederick from reaching his goal of becoming emperor. The great merchants of the city of Pisa were his allies and sent their navy to capture Frederick's ship.

As his ship was nearing the coast to put in at Ostia, the port closest to Rome, Frederick saw several of the Pisan ships coming towards him. Knowing that he would be captured if he attempted to put ashore, he turned his ship into the wind and sailed southward down the coast towards his own lands. The Pisan ships followed in pursuit. It was a race in which Frederick had only a meager head start. Was his ship lighter and swifter than the ships of the Pisan merchants? Were his sailors more skilled than theirs? The space between Frederick and the Pisans kept getting smaller. Soon the point of Monte Circeo came into view, the island where the sorceress Circe of Greek mythology had turned Ulysses' crew into swine. Would there be magic here for Frederick also? He raced for the port of Gaeta. There, just north of Naples, he would be safe. The race was close. He reached the port just before the Pisan ships reached him, and they gave up the chase.

When Frederick came ashore, the people of Gaeta were waiting for him. They couldn't believe that this young lad, running away to escape the Pisans, with no great retinue, no army of knights, no pomp or splendor, was their king. But when he finally convinced them of who he was, they provided him with the horses he needed to ride to Rome.

From Gaeta, it took Frederick a whole month to reach Rome, a journey of less than a hundred miles. Many of the guards along the road did not know that he was under the Pope's protection as his ward, and tried to prevent his passing through their region. But he was able to make his way inland further south. After many trials along the road, he arrived at Benevento, a Papal enclave. There he was recognized as a ward of the Pope and was given an escort to take him safely the rest of the way to Rome.

When Frederick arrived in Rome, he was ragged and sore but vivacious and high-spirited. The people of Rome cheered and welcomed him with open hearts, and the senators and church officials received him warmly.

Bedraggled as he was, Frederick presented himself to his guardian, Pope Innocent III. It was their first meeting. The Pope wanted to maintain control over Frederick, and Frederick wanted to maintain his freedom. They both mistrusted each other, but they also respected each other. Frederick recognized Innocent's gentility and knowledge, and Innocent admired Frederick's intelligence and spirit. Once Frederick agreed to respect the Pope's right to rule the Papal States in central Italy, the Pope was willing to support Frederick's claim to the imperial throne.

Accompanied by Archbishop Berardo, Frederick continued on his journey north with gifts from the Pope of some money and an escort. The people and senators of Rome cheered and applauded him, sending him on his way with wishes for a safe journey and success.

Frederick was now entering northern Italy on his way to Germany. He was in the territory of his enemy and rival, Otto, who would surely have alerted all his allies to Frederick's presence and given them orders to capture him and prevent him from reaching Germany. Now his journey would be truly dangerous. He would have to stay off the main roads and travel on circuitous pathways, lengthening the trip considerably. Some cities barred his way, others were indifferent to him, and others welcomed him. He was never sure how he would be received.

The city of Cremona was for him. The city of Milano was against him. As Frederick approached the Po River on his way to Cremona, a host of knights from Milano rode out to capture him. The knights of Cremona rode out to stop the Milanese knights and protect Frederick. The Milanese reached him first, but just as they closed in on him, the knights of Cremona arrived. They fought each other fiercely on the flood plain of the river. In the heat of battle, as swords flashed, men yelled, and horses reared, Frederick made his escape. He jumped on a horse and rode bareback, hard for the river. The Milanese pursued him and the Cremonese chased them. Swords rang on all sides as Frederick galloped his horse into the water, clinging to the horse's neck, as it swam across to safety. Reaching the opposite bank, he made his way alone to Cremona, riding as fast as his horse could take him. The people of the city opened the gates and cheered his arrival. They called him an angel of the Lord, as if he were a gift from heaven.

But not every city opened its gates to Frederick. It was sometimes even hard for him to get food for himself and the few remaining men of his escort. Many of his men were captured or gave up the adventure when the danger was great. Often their way was blocked because the passes over the Alps were held by Otto's army, which was still in control of Germany.

It was getting late in the year. Frederick would have to hurry now to avoid crossing the mountains in winter. The Dukes of Este and Monteferrato came to his aid and provided him with enough men for protection on the passage over the Alps. Ambushes from Otto's men were a constant danger. Because the usual passes were blocked by Otto's allies, Frederick and his new escorts climbed through the steep and narrow mountain pass near Como and Sondrio, then through the Engadine area of Switzerland. The monasteries in these mountains gave them reinforcements and hospitality.

Crossing the Alps was difficult, a challenge for any mountaineer, and this was Frederick's first experience in climbing. But he was young and determined and succeeded in the crossing, arriving safely at Lake Constance.

However, Otto and his army had arrived first and were encamped on the shore outside the city of Constance, on the border of Switzerland and Germany. The townspeople had decorated the town and, with banners flying, were preparing to open the gates to Otto and entertain him royally. At that moment Frederick arrived at the gate. He was weather-beaten and disheveled but elated and optimistic. He sent Archbishop Berardo into the city to ask for an audience with the Bishop of Constance, while he waited outside. Berardo convinced the bishop to support Frederick rather than Otto, because Otto had been excommunicated by the Pope, and the bishop persuaded the other authorities of the city to do the same.

Trumpets sounded a fanfare from the city walls, and the gates were opened to Frederick. The city counselors welcomed him and brought him into a banquet hall where the feast that had been prepared for Otto was served to Frederick. They were impressed by this young man's openness and high spirits, his clear blue eyes and genial countenance. His gentle manners and youthful self-confidence were refreshing after their dealings with the caustic Otto. Frederick had a deep understanding and mature grasp of all that they discussed. He spoke about his hatred of war and longing for peace. The city counselors were impressed by his intelligence and clear comprehension of subjects dealing with rulership and governance. They were moved by Frederick's gentleness and sincerity, and placed their hope in him as one who could bring change to a weary world.

Frederickís success in Constance was the beginning of a change in his fate. As he moved into Germany, he received the support and alliance of bishops, noblemen, dukes, counts, princes, and even kings. His retinue and escort grew as more and more knights joined him. As he visited city after city, the people's hearts were won over by his innocence and purity, and they withdrew their support for Otto. Poets honored him in their writings and in song. He was called "the innocent child of Apulia," which was one of Frederick's most beloved regions of the southern kingdom. The people told of his long and perilous journey and of how his innocence had protected him. He had shed no blood conquering his opponents. It was his good will and hopefulness that had won his followers.

The German princes elected Frederick Emperor of the Holy Roman Empire, as his father and grandfather had been. The coronation took place in the city of Mainz a few days after the election.

Frederick's youth and innocence had appeared at first to be his greatest weaknesses but turned out to be his greatest strength. His wife Constance and his court in Sicily thought that Frederick would be a lamb among wolves when he undertook his journey north. But the princes of Germany and their people accepted him as a hero and their hope for a better future. His triumph gave him tremendous confidence. Frederick sent for Constance and their son to come and join him in his great success.

But Frederick's allies and supporters held conflicting views of his success. Constance still felt that he should have held back his ambition to be greater and remained King of Southern Italy only. Archbishop Berardo was of like mind. The Pope considered that it was his Papal support that gave Frederick his victory. The King of France felt that Frederick would never have succeeded without his allegiance and help to overcome Otto's forces. The northern Italian Dukes of Monteferrato and Este were sure that Frederick would never have reached Germany without their help. But Frederick felt that it was his own ingenuity and courage that allowed him to fulfill his destiny. As a result, his self-confidence increased, and he became a commanding yet generous ruler.

In 1215, when Frederick was twenty-one years old, he attended the great Lateran Council where eight hundred representatives from western and eastern Europe confirmed his election as Holy Roman Emperor. He was crowned by the bishops and princes at Aix-la-Chapelle, the capital of the Empire and the birthplace of the first Holy Roman Emperor, Charlemagne. Following this great coronation, he traveled to Rome to be crowned by the Pope as well. This would be the second time he would meet Innocent III, in whose care he had been left when his mother died.

When Frederick and Constance arrived in Rome, they went to the Lateran Cathedral to meet Pope Innocent III. Although the Pope was very old now and would live for only another year, he was still wise as well as crafty. The young couple approached him respectfully and knelt before him to kiss the Papal ring on his finger.

"At last I meet again our dear orphan and ward of the Holy Mother Church," he said.

"Your Holiness, we are honored," they replied.

"Since you have been crowned emperor by the German princes, I too will bless your rulership and acknowledge your lordship over the Holy Roman Empire and the Kingdom of Southern Italy. But you must also vow to protect the Holy Mother Church."

"I do," Frederick answered.

"And fight against heresy, as in Provence," added Innocent, "as well as take the Holy Land from the infidel Saracens."

Frederick paused, swallowed, took a deep breath, and finally answered, "I will."

"Then I bless you, your dear wife, your offspring for generations to come, your crowns, and your kingdoms. May you rule wisely and always uphold the Church and her representatives. Go by the grace of God."

The Pope held out his white-gloved hand for them to kiss his ring again as a sign of their obedience to him. With this he dismissed them. When they had left the great hall of audience, the Pope turned to the cardinals who stood around him as witnesses to this meeting. Without looking at them, he said, "You were right. He is not much to consider, neither German nor French Norman."

"And surely not Italian," said one of the cardinals from northern Italy.

"As you said, he wouldn't fetch much in an African slave market," replied the Pope.

"But he does have many allies," said another cardinal.

"And a vast and rich realm," added another.

Innocent did not hesitate one second before he responded. "Yes, and his realm closes in our Papal States of central Italy between the Germans of the Holy Roman Empire and the southern Italians."

"This is a precarious position for Your Grace."

"I admire him," said the Pope, "but I do not trust him."

The northern Italian cardinal suggested, "Perhaps I should seek the support of the northern Lombard cities of Italy."

"Yes, they like his saddle and bit less than we do. I do not trust him at all."

The second cardinal made another recommendation, "Perhaps his promised crusade to the Holy Land will solve our problem. Perhaps the Saracens will remove him for us."

"Yes, so let us pray," responded the Pope, and then added again, "I do not trust him."

When Frederick and Constance left the hall of audience, they sighed as if they had held their breath during their whole audience with the Pope. Constance patted her brow with her handkerchief and fanned her face with it. She gave Frederick a knowing look. He smiled at her and gave a short laugh as he said, "He is an admirable prince of the Church," and rolled his eyes.

"But he made you vow to uphold his crusade against the Cathars in Provence who are also Christians. They are escaping to Italy, to your lands, even to your court to save themselves."

"The reports I receive are that the Cathars are a gentle people but criticize the Catholic Church's wealth. I uphold his crusade in word alone, not in deed."

"And your promise to crusade against the Arabs," said Constance with some exasperation. "The Arabs are part of your court, your kingdom. They are your friends."

"They are good and intelligent people," Frederick answered. "I gave my word to that old man, but he will be dead and gone before I go to war in the East." He thought for a moment, and then continued, "The Pope is a powerful man. I do not trust him."

Chapter 5

Interests in the South: Of Birds and Castles

Frederick stayed in Germany for eight years. During that time he worked with the German princes on establishing his rulership. They were fiercely independent, and Frederick had to give them many liberties to keep them loyal. He had his young son Henry crowned king with the Archbishop of Cologne as his regent. It must have been extremely difficult for Queen Constance to leave her nine-year-old son in Germany, but Frederick felt they needed to return to his beloved kingdom in southern Italy.

Soon after his return, Frederick funded the establishment of the University of Naples in 1224, one of the earliest universities to be founded in Europe. He also opened a school of medicine in Salerno. He was interested in learning about health and in keeping healthy. He even bathed daily, which was unheard of in those times. He knew that education, health, and hygiene were important for his people.

Frederick's favorite subject of study was birds. He was an avid follower of the noble art of hunting with birds, known as falconry. He studied birds in great detail, especially birds of prey, such as falcons. He traveled all over his kingdom to learn all he could from his own observations and from the knowledge of his people. He wrote to falconers in other parts of the world, especially the Arabs, and received answers to his many questions. He began to write a book in Latin about his studies in falconry called *De Arte Venandi cum Avibus*, *The Art of Hunting with Birds*. It was the first book on ornithology ever written in Europe. Frederick's studies were systematic investigations of his own, integrating information from all over the world.

With his own detailed drawings in color, the book was not only a scientific study, the first of its kind, but also a work of art. In addition to precise information on how to handle and care for the birds, Frederick covered whole pages of the manuscript with drawings and enhanced the borders of the pages with beautiful illustrations. He conveyed his zest for discovery and for the natural world in his narrations so that readers could almost see with their own eyes what Frederick saw with his. He wrote down every detail of the life, habits, and physical structure of birds, with chapters on their feathers, beaks, weights, wing spans, talons, eyes, and digestive systems.

He drew many other kinds of birds besides hunting falcons and hawks, including owls, eagles, doves, storks, larks, swallows, pheasants, parrots, pelicans, vultures, swans, and ducks. He also drew the scenery of the countryside in which the birds lived. He added little details like a fox with a lively eye and tail watching birds from a thicket, or men fishing near a group of waterfowl, or someone swimming in a lake to retrieve a duck that was caught by his falcon, or a boy climbing a tree toward a nest full of eggs, or a picnic with lunch being cooked on an open fire. He drew the falconers and their equipment. He drew them on foot and illustrated how to mount a horse, correctly and incorrectly, with a falcon on one's wrist. He described and illustrated how to calm a bird by stroking it the right way and breathing gently on it. His pictures of falconers show how they dressed in those days, what colors they wore, their gloves and hats, and how they wore their hair under tight caps.

Researching and writing his book gave Frederick such pleasure and solace that it became a retreat from the world of politics and war and

Fig. 4. Frederick writing and illustrating his book

disharmony in personal affairs. He carried his book with him wherever he traveled, referring to it, adding to it, sharing it with others. He worked on it for thirty years. It was one of his greatest treasures.

One of the names that his people used to describe Frederick was *Il Stupor Mundi,* which means "the Wonder of the World." Another name by which he was known was *Puer Apulia,* which means "Child of Apulia." Apulia is the English word for the region of Italy known as Puglia. It is the southeastern part of the peninsula, the spur and heel of the Italian boot.

Frederick was raised in Sicily and his capital city, Palermo, was in Sicily. But one of his favorite parts of his realm was Puglia. It has long stretches of seashore, flat plains, high plateaus, and a few rolling hills. It was easy to travel through Puglia on horseback. It was rich in farmlands. In Frederick's time Puglia was covered with extensive forests, especially oak forests, which offered places to observe birds.

He enjoyed practicing the art of falconry there. He had a fondness for the people of Puglia, who also showed him great honor. It was there that he found the perfect hill on which to build his most famous castle, Castel Del Monte.

Frederick had one cathedral built during his life. It was presented as a gift to his faithful subjects in the city of Altamura in Puglia. On the other hand, he had many, many castles built all over his realm. They were of various sizes and different designs, and they are found on mountain tops and on the seashore alike. His castles, fortresses, citadels, and palaces number over two hundred. His creative genius shone in its most dazzling light in architecture. Many of his castles were square with square towers. Some had round towers. Some seemed to be pleasure palaces and hunting lodges rather than defensive structures, as were most medieval castles.

On a gently rising hill, eighteen hundred feet high above the plain of Puglia, stands Castel Del Monte. The landscape is sparse, broad and calm. There are few houses to be seen in an ocean of silvery green olive trees. Many of them are *trulli*, small farm houses and field houses for storing tools and for overnight stays during the harvest time when there is lots of work to be done. These strange little houses set the scene for the castle on the mount. They are made out of white stones stacked up to form a round room with a stone roof shaped like a cone, coming to a point on top. The hill is crowned with a dark green forest of pine trees, above which stands the white castle looking like an emperor's crown made out of crystal.

This was the last and most beautiful castle that Frederick built. But why he built it and for what purpose are mysteries even today. It is an octagon with an octagonal courtyard and octagonal towers at the eight corners. It is the geometric marvel of the Middle Ages. There are two stories with the same number of rooms on each of the floors, sixteen rooms in all, shaped like trapezoids. Some rooms have fireplaces, and some have bathrooms with running water, a feature highly unusual for the Middle Ages. The doorways lead from one room to the next and from one floor to the next through octagonal towers with spiral staircases creating the effect of a labyrinth. The sculptural details that remain, the remnants of mosaic flooring, and the rosy and vermillion colored stones reveal that Frederick created a beautiful work of art.

But why did he build it? It is not really a fortress because it has windows in the outer walls that are too big to defend properly, and the slit windows in the towers, too small to shoot arrows through, are only useful for allowing light to enter the spiral staircases. There are no battlements on the roof. There is no protecting curtain wall or moat surrounding the castle, and no drawbridge to guard the front door. It has no bastions projecting from the walls. There is no space to provide for the needs of a garrison of soldiers, no barracks, no stables, no storerooms or armory, and no kitchens.

Could it have been a hunting lodge or a pleasure palace? It seems too elaborate a building in its shape and layout to be a hunting lodge and is too huge, dense, and severe to be a pleasure palace. There is a throne room but no real reception hall. There are bathrooms but no real kitchen. There are fireplaces in some of the rooms but not all. Was he merely attempting to design an ideal piece of architectural art, to make an artistic statement? We know that Frederick's many interests brought some of the greatest minds of Europe to his court. He gathered together the best architects, mathematicians, musicians, astronomers, and scholars of his time. Could the castle be simply an embodiment of all these facets of Frederick's creative spirit?

The front door of Castel del Monte faces due east. Therefore the castle was placed in space in a deliberate manner. On the east-facing wall of the inner courtyard on its upper story is a rectangle cut in the stone so that it is recessed a few inches. This indented rectangle would not appear noteworthy to the casual observer upon entering the courtyard. But, on the first day of spring, the vernal equinox around March 21st, and on the first day of fall, the autumnal equinox around September 21st, the rectangle reveals its purpose. The light of the sun rising in the east passes through the window on the second floor above the front door. It goes through the throne room and out the door-like window that overlooks the courtyard on the opposite side of the room. It strikes the east-facing wall of the courtyard right in the middle of that rectangle. During the course of the year the light moves across the rectangle, reaching its outer edge on one side on the winter solstice, the first day of winter and the shortest day of the year, around December 21st. It reaches the opposite outer edge on the summer solstice, the first day of summer and the longest day of the year, around June 21st. So the rectangle acts as a visual calendar, marking the changes of the seasons with the light of the sun, which means that the castle was designed with a knowledge of astronomy.

This castle of mysteries also has an order of numbers embodied in it and an inherent geometry. The front doorway stands within a star-shaped pentagon, the form in which the human being can stand with arms and legs outreaching. The measurement of the Divine Proportion or Golden Ratio, the well-known ratio 1.618, is found in many places throughout the castle. The eight-pointed star or compass rose is the ground plan for the castle. The eight-pointed star was described in Leonardo Fibonacci's book *Practica Geometriae* as a proportional arrangement applied in planning cities. Fibonacci met the Emperor Frederick at his court, and he dedicated his book *Liber Quadratum*, *The Book of Squares*, to Frederick. Leonardo Fibonacci is famous for having introduced to Europe the Arabic numbers that we use today, as well as for his number sequence: 1, 1, 2, 3, 5, 8, 13 ... , which appears throughout nature but is especially visible in the growth patterns of plants and shells. It is also found in the Golden Ratio which is present in things as diverse as the human body and all the arts.

The Castel Del Monte is a combination of classical Greek, Romanesque, and Gothic elements in architecture. The form has the Arabic design of the octagon star, and the construction is clearly influenced by the Cistercians, a monastic order founded in France and very influential in Italy. The Cistercian monks had great practical knowledge that advanced agriculture and architecture in the Middle

Ages. They were greatly favored by Frederick, and he became a lay brother of their order. The combination of Arab-Islamic and Cistercian-European characteristics makes Castel Del Monte a unique building. It could be considered a temple built by Frederick and dedicated to the Liberal Arts, the seven branches of learning considered essential by scholars of the Middle Ages: grammar, logic, rhetoric, arithmetic, geometry, music, and astronomy. He may have built it as a gathering place for the great teachers of those times in his "temple of learning."

Fig. 5. Castel Del Monte

Fig. 6. Illustration from Frederick's Book of Falconry

Fig. 7. Illustration from Frederick's Book of Falconry

deste uolable et qui na par
sul terre, se ne die une qnecou
et deste uolauf sent orfuuf.
Toute uoie pur ancune acoul
tumance que nour auons ete
entr la chace des ousauf et p
aucune transsumption de par
ler nour auonr deuise entr
les aquariques et terrestres
les morens ousauf, lequel sh
plus leger plus contra uner
uolant et demeurent en laur.
et ont signorie en la counpr
ou de lor matiere les hautes
chosef et les darrieres des lign
ers demanf de routes ces chp
ses dorons none exemple en
pursiuanf la diuision delles
selonc los diuerses menieres
et selonc los diuerses sem oia
cef. Des ousauf deuaue ba r
demeurent con vios es iaues
qui ne se departent point ne
pour uiande ne pour autre
chose auis que tantque au
cune foif elles se muent du
ne pane en autre ou pour ce
quelles muent los leuf selonc

la mutation des tens ainsi
con sont une meniere de ratrof
et coubians de mere qui sont
apelez plauon et cigne, et cil q
Aristotes apelle en luure des bel
tes pellicans qui en puille loie
apelet cossun se sont ousel asir
et blanc en la cruete de cig
nes elles ont loue et large boc
desotz lequel elles ont une pe
lette quelles couurent et ciotne
en peschant ou mehuent de uai
se et ont dons de piez conu au
tres, ils cauns genuue le doi dar
ner as dous denatuers, la qle
chose namene point as autres
ousauf qui ont les piez henu
auf est et mis dautre pru ou
nuant se depurtent del uues,
la autre nont pas con tor los
mansion ens iaues, mais se
departent pour les deu, doꝛel
desus dites cest asouoir pour
aler dune pane en autre ꝑ
muer loꝛ les selonc la mun
aon de tens et encor sen depur
tent pour querir loꝛ uiande
et pour ce que los nature te

Fig. 8. Illustration from Frederick's Book of Falconry

Chapter 6

𝒯he 𝒞avalcade and the 𝒞afun

Frederick's court was in the capital city of Palermo, Sicily, but he often traveled around his kingdom in a cavalcade, a parade of horsemen and wagons. He would go to a town where he had one of his castles and stay for a while before moving on to the next one. He would write to the mayor of the town in which he would be staying next to let him know when he would arrive.

When he was ready to leave, he sent his couriers ahead to the next town so that the townspeople could also prepare for his arrival. The gates of all the towns were opened to Frederick and his retinue in the name of the emperor. Riding into the main piazza with banners flying from the tops of their lances and their horses' hooves pounding the stones of the street, the couriers announced to the mayor, nobles, and townspeople that the royal cavalcade would soon arrive. There would be a number of days in which to prepare. The couriers read a list of what would be needed during the emperor's stay. The emperor and his court would reside in his castle, but every available house that had room to spare would be needed for his retinue, and, still, many would have to camp outside the town. The emperor would pay the farmers for miles around to send their produce to feed the visitors. The butchers would be busy preparing the meat from the flocks and herds that would be brought to them. Fuel for cooking and heating would be needed in abundance, as well as fodder for the animals of the cavalcade. Barrels of wine by the hundreds would be delivered in advance.

On the day of Frederick's expected arrival, the town would be in a bustle of activity. The townsfolk ran to the walls and gateway when the first few riders came into view. These were the heralds, arriving in advance with flags waving and trumpets blaring. The excitement mounted as the people waited for the emperor's arrival. The mayor practiced his welcoming speech. The captain of the guards had his men polishing their armor. The streets were swept and watered. Women baked mountains of bread. Children ran around, shouting to each other.

But what of the simple countryfolk, the peasants, working in their fields when Frederick's cavalcade passed by? What did they think when they looked up from their work and saw the dust in the sky? Was it the dust of an invading army? Who could it be? Were they safe or in danger? What did they think, not knowing what this massive parade, this army of travelers, was?

Imagine how Giuseppe, Ciccio, Minguccio, Luigi, and Rocco, watching from the roadside, wondered at the cavalcade passing them. Minguccio was the first to reach the small hill above the road. He stood there in utter amazement. This was the most glorious sight he had ever seen in his life. His friends, running with their hoes still in their hands, arrived from the fields, one after the other. Each was dressed in homespun pants and a simple shirt of linen; they were barefoot and wore straw hats of varying sizes and shapes. They appeared to be dull-witted country bumpkins of the most awkward, unpolished, graceless kind. They were simple but good, kind-hearted men, one a dolt, another a simpleton, the next an oaf, the following one a nincompoop, and the last a blockhead of the finest sort. They were what is known as *cafone* in Italian, or *cafun* in their dialect.

Giuseppe came up to Minguccio and called him, "*Uè*, Mingucc'," and when he didn't answer, he yelled, "*Oa*, Mingucc'!", and slapped his friend on the back to get his attention.

"*Uè*, Giusepp'," responded Minguccio, without taking his eyes off the marvelous parade.

"*E c'e fai?* And what are you doing?" asked Giuseppe, lifting his shoulders and chin, bringing his fingers together, pointing upward, artichoke-like.

"Counting."

"You can count?" Giuseppe asked jokingly. "What are you counting?"

"*I muli.*"

"What mules?"

"*A basch!* Down there!" bawled Minguccio, shooting his arms out, palms up, to point. "*Cento quaranta nove* … a hundred forty-nine."

At that moment, little Ciccio and big burly Rocco lumbered up to them. Having heard what his friends had just said, Ciccio asked, "Rocco, *dove*, where, Rocco?"

"*A basch*, in the valley, Ciccio," said Rocco with his hands held behind his back, pointing with his chin.

"*Uè*, Rocco!" called Luigi as he ran up, the last to arrive. "*Chi è questo?* Who is this?" he asked, waving his arms back and forth.

Rocco took his hands from behind his back, opened his arms wide, and declared regally, "*Il Imperatore Federico!* With his cavalcade, *Guarda*. Look, Luig'."

"*Madonn', c'e bell'*. Madonna, that's beautiful, Mingucc'," said the astonished Ciccio.

Minguccio responded with, "*Stupendo, cento cinquanti muli,* Giusepp'. It's stupendous, a hundred fifty mules."

Giuseppe tried to draw his friend's attention away from the mules to the regal figure of the emperor. "Mingucc', *guarda*, Federico in the front, *Il Stupor Mundi*, the Wonder of the World."

"Ciccio, he's magnificent … the horse … he's riding. The horse is magnificent!"

"Rocco, Rocco, *che grande il Imperator.*"

"*Si, uè* Luig', look at his bodyguards, *i Saraceni*, Arab archers, *che colore*, what colors!"

"*Oa*, Rocco, look at the soldiers," cried Luigi, pointing and holding his hand up high over his head. "*I Germani grandi* — the big Germans." Then, holding his hand down at shoulder height, he added, "*Italiani.*"

"*Uè, Siciliani, Luig', Siciliani.*" Rocco corrected him. "Sicilians."

"*Si, si, Siciliani cavaliere*, knights," agreed Ciccio, wagging his head up and down.

Minguccio returned to the animals, his greatest interest. "*I animali, Giusepp'.*"

"*Chi*, who? *I Siciliani*?"

"*No, i animali!* Look, Ciccio, what's that?"

"*Un elefante*, Mingucc'."

"*Comè*, what?"

"*Che grande naso*, what a big nose! Like you, Rocco!"

"*Che grandi 'recchi*, what big ears! *Come te*, Ciccio!"

"*I questi*, Mingucc', *chi sono questi*? Who are these?" asked the astonished Ciccio, staring wide-eyed at an animal he'd never seen before.

"*Boh!?* Got me! Who knows? Not me!" was Minguccio's answer, as he raised his shoulders up and held his hands out, palms up.

But Giuseppe knew. "*Camels*, Mingucc', camels."

"Bravo, *bravo*, Giusepp'."

"Look at those *grandi gatti*, large cats, Luig'."

"*Leopardi*, Rocco. Leopards for hunting," explained Luigi.

"*Uè*, Ciccio, there's your sister," said Rocco, replacing his hands behind his back and acting as if there was nothing unusual in what he had said.

"*Dovè*, where?" asked Ciccio.

"That's a monkey," corrected Minguccio, "more monkeys, and ..." Then Ciccio realized that Rocco was teasing him by calling the monkey his sister.

"*Mannagg'*, darn!" yelled Ciccio, hitting Minguccio over the head with his hat. Rocco ducked away and laughed at him.

"*Oa*, Mingucc'. *Senti ai musichisti con tromba e tambor.* Listen to the musicians with trumpet and drum," said Giuseppe. Then they all together began to imitate the musicians, their hands holding invisible trumpets to their lips and their fists pounding invisible drums. They marched in place, bringing their knees up ridiculously high, almost falling over backwards, and merrily singing at the top of their lungs.

"Bah, bah, badah, dah, dum, dah, dum, dah. Bah, bah, badah, dah, dum ..." Then they stopped one after the other in wide-eyed silence, leaning forward, their hands hanging at their sides, their mouths hanging open. Then all at once, all together, they sighed, "*Che bell'*, what beauty! *Che bell' signorini*, what beautiful young ladies! *I ballarini*, the dancing girls!"

"*Si*," said Giuseppe. "Yes, the emperor's dancing girls."

"Giusepp', *che belle face!* What beautiful faces!" sighed Minguccio, stroking his cheek with his hand.

"Mingucc', *che bell' petti!* What beautiful breasts," sighed Ciccio, making two cups out of his hands and holding them up to his chest.

"Ciccio, *che bell' pancia!* What a beautiful belly," sighed Rocco, stroking his big pot belly with both his hands and closing his eyes with delight.

"Rocco, *che bell' culo!* What a beautiful behind," sighed Luigi, rubbing his own behind and raising his eyes to heaven. Then, putting their hands together as if they were praying and waving them up and down at the wrists, they crooned all together, "*Che bell' donne, Madonn' mia!* What beautiful women, my Lady!" And they stared. And they stared. They stared until it seemed their eyes would fall out.

They had never seen such beauty. And as they stared, one by one their wives came up behind them. Giuseppe got a kick in the pants from his darling Marietta which sent him running. Minguccio got his ear pulled by his chubby Angelina as she dragged him away. Big Rocco's petite, sweet Filomena grabbed him around the waist, picked him right up off the ground and carried him off. Rosalia, Ciccio's adorable wife, kissed his cheek. He slowly turned his head to find out who kissed him, but he could not take his eyes off the beauties. Then he felt a tap on his shoulder, and finally looked right into Rosalia's face. She gave him a smack with her hand that sent him reeling. Poor Luigi heard the smack and looked around, expecting to see Ciccio. Instead he saw his own dainty, dear Brunella with a wooden spoon in her hand, tapping her foot and looking at him with enough fire in her eyes to melt him on the spot. He sheepishly smiled at her, then slowly turned his head to look back at the cavalcade. She gave him a rap on the head with her spoon that sent him flying. She kept after him, waving her spoon over his head until he had run all the way back to his field. Then she stormed off.

Luigi realized he had left his hoe where he had been standing to watch the marvelous parade. He went back to get it once Brunella was out of sight. He found Giuseppe, Minguccio, Ciccio and Rocco all there, also picking up their forgotten hoes. They were all craning their necks in hopes of getting another look at the beautiful dancing girls as they rode off in their silken, covered litters. But right behind them came their wives again, running, which sent them scurrying like a pack of startled rabbits.

"*Che bell', Mingucc'.*"

"*Si, bellissima, Giusepp'.*"

"*No, no, è stato meraviglioso!* It was wonderful!"

"*Si, certo, Ciccio, stupendo!* For sure, stupendous!"

"*Aspetta me! Aspetta me!* Wait for me," yelled Luigi, trying to catch up with them, legs wheeling, and looking over his shoulder at Brunella.

Yes, the emperor traveled in a grand style. Frederick and his courtiers, mounted guards, and soldiers all rode magnificent Spanish and Arabian horses. Mules and camels were used as pack animals, carrying heavy loads of supplies. He also brought leopards and falcons for hunting, and a whole zoo of unusual beasts such as bears, lions, lynxes, panthers, apes, and a great assortment of birds, ostriches, eagles, hawks, vultures, owls, and peacocks. The common folk had never seen many of these animals, especially the wonderful elephant that Frederick received as a gift from an Arabian sultan. The people were delighted with this spectacle, and they continued to gaze and marvel as long as the emperor stayed in town. He was delighted to give his people a glimpse of the wide world.

The townspeople also learned much from their encounters with the people in Frederick's retinue: the big, blonde German soldiers who came with him from the north, the dark-faced, colorfully dressed, tall Saracens who made up his guard, the Greeks with flowing Byzantine robes. Frederick had many musicians to entertain him, his courtiers, and his hosts, but they also played and sang for the local people, creating a series of traveling concerts by the Italians, or the troubadours from Provence, or the Arab ensembles. There were dancing girls who also entertained as acrobats. Dressed in saffron and scarlet-dyed silks with little bells strung around their hips, they enchanted the crowds with their graceful movements. Besides seeing all these visitors from far away with their exotic dress and manners, the people also heard songs in all the different languages and the music of all the different cultures. A whole new world opened up for them when the emperor came to town.

Chapter 7

A Meeting with a Saint

Frederick's life was full of conflicts with the Church. In 1209, for example, Pope Innocent forbade the study of the works of the Greek philosopher Aristotle. But Michael Scotus made translations of Aristotle from the Arabic sources and dedicated them to Frederick. Also, Francis of Assisi was preaching the virtues of poverty all the while the Church in Rome was one of the wealthiest institutions in Europe. And later Pope Gregory had the Franciscans preach against Frederick's right to be emperor.

One of Frederick's castles was in the city of Bari on the Adriatic coast of Puglia. It was there that the tale of his meeting with Francis of Assisi originated.

"Ah, Michael Scotus (Michael of Scotland), you are my court astrologer, mathematician, alchemist, and excellent translator of Hebrew, Arabic, and Greek. You certainly are a wise man. Tell me. Is it not true that my people love me?"

"They call you their beloved child from southern Italy, *Puer Apulia.*"

"The Germans welcomed me. My Italian subjects praise me. The Moslems respect me. Even the people of Rome welcome me. Only the Pope and his allies in the northern Italian cities oppose me."

"Federico, the Pope has decreed that if you do not carry out your vowed crusade against the Moslems in the Holy Land, he will excommunicate you, throw you out of the grace of the Church. And, unless they denounce you, he will excommunicate all your subjects as well."

"I will go to the Middle East, but not because I am afraid of his Bull[1] of Excommunication. I would like to meet some of the Moslem rulers with whom I have been exchanging letters."

"Oh yes, a gift has arrived from Ashrof, the Sultan of Damascus. It is a silver globe, a planetarium, constructed with admirable skill. On it the figures of the sun and moon indicate the hours of day and night in the course of their movements. A truly beautiful and useful gift."

"Wonderful! You must send him the polar bear from my zoo."

"You have also received letters from falconers and bird watchers from the Middle East, one from North Africa, and another from a place far to the northwest, Greenland."

"Marvelous! Let me see them right away."

"Speaking of a crusade to the East ... there is a monk here from Assisi in Umbria, one called Francis, who is on a pilgrimage. He would speak with you about the Pope. He is famous for his piety."

"That is rare among monks these days. They are usually no holier than I am. I will not speak to him until we test his piety. We shall tempt him. If he overcomes the temptation, then I will speak with him. Send for lovely Fatima, the dancing girl."

Fatima was summoned and arrived dressed in silken veils. She was lithe and shapely, with flashing dark eyes and a winning smile. Because she was little, the emperor had to lean over to whisper his instructions to her. He wanted her to dance her most alluring dance for Francis. Fatima bowed gracefully and assured Frederick that she would use all her charms.

Francis was waiting in a small hall. Frederick and Michael Scotus stood listening, behind a door concealed by a tapestry. Francis sat

---

1. A "Bull" is an official Papal document or decree.

quietly in prayer, waiting for his audience with the emperor. Suddenly the monk heard the music of a ney (flute) and dumbeck (drum) from an adjoining room, and, instead of the emperor, in came Fatima, gliding and smiling. She danced in front of Francis. She danced around him. She came as close as she could, almost touching him, but he continued in his prayers. She stroked his cheek and the back of his neck, but she could not move him. She danced slowly and sensually. She danced quickly and lightly, springing into a back walkover. But not one of her seductive movements distracted Francis from his prayers. Then, without a word, he untied his rope belt from around his waist. He got up from his chair slowly and folded the rope in half. He watched her dance for another moment and then began to flail at her with his rope belt. Fatima screamed, the musicians stopped playing, and the lovely dancer ran away from Francis before he could reach her. Francis returned in peace to his seat and to his prayers.

Frederick and Michael smiled and nodded to each other as Fatima approached them. Frederick complimented her on her exquisite performance and gave her a gold necklace as a reward. She smiled at him, bowed deeply, and returned to the harem (women's apartments), swaying gracefully as she walked away. Frederick asked Michael to bring Francis to him in his dining room. There the two great men met and had a long conversation. At last, Francis said, "I preach to the people, and the Pope would have me and my brothers preach to them against you."

"If the Pope were as poor and as pious as you, Francis, I would obey him, but ..."

"I also preach to the birds, Your Majesty."

"I observe the birds, my fine monk, *for the truest worship of God is to know His works. I have always questioned and doubted. Only by courageously questioning can a man rise to his full stature.*"

And with that they said farewell and parted ways.

Fig. 9. Fatima and Francis

Chapter 8

A Meeting with the Wise Men

After Frederick's meeting with Francis, he may have made his next stop nearby at Andria, a city that was devoted to him. In the countryside near Andria was his Castel Del Monte. Frederick called for a meeting to be held in the castle of all the greatest scholars and teachers of his kingdom and from other parts of the world. Hebrew scholars, Moslem scientists and mathematicians, Greek philosophers, and people of great learning gathered from all over Europe. They were encamped around the castle, coming together each day to discuss the profound questions that Frederick put to them. They would meet in various rooms, each one of which was dedicated to one of the liberal arts. At night, lying on cushions in the octagonal courtyard to observe the starry heavens, they would discuss the attributes of the constellations.

One day Michael Scotus approached Frederick. "My lord," he said, "as you asked me, I have translated from the Arabic the works on biology and zoology of the Greek philosopher Aristotle."

"Excellent, Michael," replied Frederick. "Are all our great guests gathered? I look forward to meeting them and knowing their minds, whether they be Christian, Moslem, or Jew."

"Your Majesty, there are also are scholars from Baghdad, translators from Spain, and philosophers from Syria, all of whom have brought falconers at your request."

"Wonderful, Michael," said the emperor. "Let us go in and begin this meeting of great minds."

Frederick addressed the assembly of men with a philosophical introduction to their meeting: *"One should accept as truth only that which is proved by force of reason and by nature."*

To this they all replied, "On this point of view our learning is based."

Then Michael Scotus began to introduce the guests to the emperor.

"Here is your representative from the university that you established in Naples."

"Ah, Filippo!" said Frederick.

"My lord," he answered, bowing.

"How fares the student from Aquino? Has he proven worthy?"

"Thomas Aquinas[2] is one of our finest scholars and succeeds in his studies."

"Excellent, Filippo. And how is the medical school in Salerno?"

"The licensing of doctors goes well, and the studies of human anatomy and physiology also proceed well."

"Excellent. *It is science and not faith alone that will open the future for us,*" said Frederick.

Then another scholar was introduced, Leonardo Fibonacci from Pisa, who introduced the Arabic numbers to Europe replacing the old Roman numerals.

"Leonardo Fibonacci, my dear friend of numbers. Thank you for bringing the Arabic numerals to the university."

"My lord, I am working on studies in algebra and geometry that will interest you greatly."

"Marvelous. Leonardo, I want you to meet my court mathematician, John of Palermo, and the Egyptian mathematician al-Hanifi. I would like

---

2. Thomas Aquinas (1225–1274) was the greatest philosopher, scholar, and theologian of the medieval Catholic Church.

to propose a tournament among you all, a mathematical tournament. I will set you some problems on which I have been working."

"My lord, the Pope questions your communing with foreign scholars," said Leonardo Fibonacci.

With a knavish smile, Frederick said, "I would like to pose some questions to His Grace, the Pope," to which Fibonacci retorted, "I doubt His Grace would have a stomach for your questions, let alone a mind to answer them. Give us an example of one of your problems, please!"

"*How is it that the soul of a living man which has passed away to another life than ours cannot be induced to return?*"

The assembled scholars all murmured their approval of this question, and asked for another.

"*Where are Hell, Purgatory, and Heaven? What is God's precise location in the heavenly spheres? And exactly how does He sit on His throne? What do the angels and saints do in His presence?* I would like a precise answer from the Pope."

"The Pope claims infallibility, but he may not have precise answers," mused Fibonacci.

To each question that Frederick put to them, the scholars responded with words of affirmation, laughter, and requests for more questions.

"Gentlemen, what about volcanoes, geysers? Why is the water of the ocean and seas salty? And what of the earth itself? Does it have a hollow space at its center? Or is it solid throughout?"

The scholars requested that Frederick tell them about his own work as it related to their particular interests. Frederick assured them that he would share his knowledge with them, since, as he said, "*Such treasures of the mind ought not to be hoarded but given freely to all people, since all people desire knowledge.*"

"My lord, tell us of how you tied ribbons to the tails of fish to study their migration."

"My lord, tell us of your work on problems of optics and physics."

"My lord, show us your new designs for hourglasses to tell time."

"And of water pumps and suits to allow us to go underwater to study the sea beds."

"My lord, show us how your book on falconry progresses."

"And your study of horses and their breeding, as well as the breeding of camels."

Requests, questions, answers, discussions, and conversation continued into the wee hours of the morning. Frederick brought the meeting to a close by bidding them all a good night in each of their native languages, and concluded by saying, "*As for myself, all of the time that is not occupied with affairs of state, I spend in reading, that my mind may become an instrument for the acquisition of knowledge, without which there can be no free and liberal life for humanity.*"

Fig. 10. Frederick standing with his book

Chapter 9

Problems with the Popes

Four Popes came to power during Frederick's lifetime. He always hoped that after the death of one, the next would be reasonable toward him. But it was never the case. The Popes proclaimed many of Frederick's actions wrong or evil, but their motivation for doing so was fear. Because Frederick ruled the lands both to the north and south of the Papal States in central Italy, each Pope in turn felt insecure in the control of his borders and neighbors. Nevertheless, the independent spirit of some of the northern Italian cities supplied the Popes with ready allies in their opposition to Frederick.

Frederick's troubles began when he promised Pope Innocent III he would go on a crusade to the Holy Land. He put it off for fifteen years. Pope Honorius III, who succeeded Innocent, tolerated this delay, but when Pope Gregory IX took the Papal throne, he excommunicated Frederick for not keeping his crusader's vow. Although he was no longer allowed to go on a crusade because he had been expelled from the Church, Frederick defied Gregory and went anyway. So Pope Gregory, having excommunicated him once for not going, now excommunicated him a second time because he went after all! Frederick was therefore not welcomed by some of the other crusaders when he arrived in Jerusalem.

Frederick was the only crusader who did not fight the Moslems. Instead, he made a ten-year truce with al-Kamil, the Sultan of Cairo. He was able to do this because he had grown up among the Moslems of Sicily, who were subjects of his kingdom. He spoke their language and appreciated their knowledge and culture. His peaceful truce made it possible for him to enter Jerusalem, and there he crowned himself king of that holy city.

Pope Gregory, in his fury at what he considered a brazen act of defiance, excommunicated the whole city. Then he had a rumor spread throughout Italy that Frederick was dead and attacked his lands in southern Italy. Emperor Frederick hurried home from the Holy Land. When he arrived, his people rejoiced and drove the Papal armies out. Frederick led his army to Rome, where the people welcomed him. He did not drive out Pope Gregory, but asked for peace, which the Pope granted.

Frederick lived in peace with the Church until the new Pope, Innocent IV, deposed Frederick the Emperor, and declared a crusade against him. Frederick wrote to the kings of Europe asking them for their support, warning them that the Pope could do the same to any of them. Frederick declared that the Pope's work was to save the souls of Christians, while his own duty as emperor was to protect and rule his people justly. The Pope attacked the emperor's authority and his character in every way possible. He sent out Papal bulls to churches throughout Europe announcing that Frederick was no longer emperor in the eyes of the Church. He ordered all the bishops, priests, and monks to preach against Frederick, although not all obeyed him, at the risk of excommunication. The Pope was relentless in his efforts to overthrow Frederick.

Finally, the Pope and his cardinals came to the conclusion that there could be no real peace as long as Frederick ruled. He must be dealt with. "We are at war with Moslems, and he protects and supports them," began the Pope. One after another, the cardinals added their comments.

"And he has Saracen bodyguards."

"He keeps a harem like the infidel sultans."

"He has made laws to protect and support Moslem merchants."

"And Jewish merchants."

The Pope interrupted them and changed the subject. "Frederick's court is the richest in all of Christendom." He paused, and then added, "And the most sinful. Scholars indeed! What have he and his so-called scholars learned?"

"He suffocated a man by sealing him in a barrel in hopes of seeing his soul leave at death."

To this Frederick would have explained that the man was a condemned criminal. Rather than put him to death by hanging as the law required, he had him sealed in a barrel. As a scientist, Frederick reasoned that his death contributed to knowledge rather than just satisfying the hangman's rope.

But another cardinal went on. "He disemboweled two men after they had eaten a big meal, one having slept and the other having exercised. He wanted to see which one digested his meal better. Can you believe such barbarism?"

To this Frederick would have described how it was that these two men also were condemned criminals, and that the one who slept did indeed digest his meal better, and that by this Frederick learned something valuable about digestion.

Then another cardinal told this remarkable tale: "He had an orphaned child cared for but no one was allowed to speak to the child. He wanted to discover its mother tongue. Can you imagine? He wanted to know if the primary language of all people would be Hebrew or Greek or Arabic or Latin." But Frederick never discovered what the primary language was. The infant died from being deprived of speech, which is necessary for all people to thrive.

The Pope continued to report on the emperor's failings. "He gave the city of Lucera in southern Italy to his Sicilian Saracens, complete with mosques in which to worship their infidel god. Whose side is he on?"

Frederick would have answered that he was on the side of his subjects, regardless of their ethnic background or religion. When his Saracen subjects were in revolt in Sicily, he offered to move them by the thousands to Puglia. He built the city of Lucera for them, and set up workshops for cloth production to support them. Ever after they were faithful to him and formed his bodyguard and the core of his standing army.

But the cardinals continued to find fault with him.

"He bathes daily!"

"Even on Sunday, the Lord's day of rest!"

The Pope ended the discussion by declaring that Frederick was the Anti-Christ. Then he added, "There can be no peace for the Church as long as Frederick is emperor."

The Pope was afraid that Frederick would invade Rome and capture him. To avoid that risk, Pope Innocent fled to the city of Lyon in France. There, at a council of the Church fathers, he declared Frederick deposed. But that did not stop Frederick from ruling his lands, for he had more supporters than the Pope. He would rule until his dying day.

Chapter 10

Many Wives and Many Children

What can we know about the personal life of an emperor? What do we know about his marriages and his children? Frederick wed four times. His first three wives were chosen for him by the Pope. He married them out of duty, for political reasons and for the sake of his kingdom, although it is clear that he did love Constance. It is hard to know whether there developed a sincere love for the two wives who came after Constance. The main objective of these marriages was to produce a legitimate heir to the throne.

Frederick certainly did enjoy the company of women. He maintained a harem that he inherited from his Norman ancestors, who, when they took over the kingdom of Sicily from the Moslems, also continued the ancient Moslem custom of providing quarters for certain women of the court. Frederick had many children, perhaps as many as twelve. Four of them were legitimate heirs. Did he love them more than his illegitimate children? Did he love them all equally, both the boys and the girls? How much time was he able to give them and their mothers in the course of his duties as a ruler?

These are questions that leave us wondering. History tells us about a person's deeds. It tells us very little about a person's thoughts and feelings. It is hard to imagine how much love, appreciation, or interest Frederick had in his intimate relationships. As a ruler he faced his subjects with one visage, but what was his countenance like when he turned to his family?

In 1209, when Frederick was fifteen years old, Pope Innocent III arranged his marriage to Constance of Aragon, widow of the king of Hungary. It was his hope that Frederick's youthful vigor would be bridled by his being wedded to a woman ten years older. From the reports he had received about her, he expected her to be religious, faithful to the Church, and obedient to Papal authority, but he was very mistaken. Constance was Frederick's loving wife and supported him fully, giving up her only son Henry VII. Whether she did so willingly or not, it was a great sacrifice. Henry was their first and only child. When he was only six years old, he was elected king by the German princes. When Frederick was sure that his son was secure on the throne, he left Henry, an eight-year-old boy, in Germany and returned with Constance to their kingdom in southern Italy.

But at the age of twenty-four, Henry rebelled against his father. He joined the Pope, some of the northern Italian cities, and some German princes in a plot to overthrow his father's authority in the Holy Roman Empire. Frederick immediately went to Germany with a small group of knights. His son's supporters fled, leaving Henry to face his father. He begged for mercy, but Frederick, his heart broken at finding that his son was not trustworthy, was pitiless. Frederick removed Henry from the throne and sent him to southern Italy where he was placed under house arrest in one of Frederick's castles in Calabria. Henry pined away in his confinement, and, not long after, died when his horse rode off a cliff. Whether the horse slipped or whether Henry deliberately rode off the cliff to end his life was never clear. Frederick's heart was broken once again by the news of the death of his son, his first child.

But that was just the first of Frederick's heartaches. Constance, in her mid-thirties and still beautiful with her long, fair hair, was in failing health and died after thirteen years of marriage. She was truly an empress, and her husband treated her in life and death with love, gratitude, and respect. Frederick had Constance's body wrapped in a splendid crimson robe embroidered with gold and pearls, and entombed her in a beautiful sarcophagus in the cathedral in Palermo. He placed a magnificent jewel-covered diadem in her tomb, a gift taken from his head but given with his heart.

Three years later, Frederick married again. Again, it was an arranged marriage for political reasons, designed by Pope Honorius III and John of Briene, the father of the bride-to-be. John was a crusader whose wife had inherited the crown of the Kingdom of Jerusalem, a kingdom that had been created by the crusaders after they seized it from the Moslems. When John of Briene's wife died, he wanted his daughter to inherit her mother's crown as queen of Jerusalem, with Frederick as king. The Pope thought that if Frederick married Jolanda of Briene, he would fulfill his crusader's vow and go off to the Holy Land to fight. Frederick thought that adding King of Jerusalem to his other titles of Emperor of the Holy Roman Empire and King of Sicily would be grand. He also knew that such a title would be helpful for diplomatic reasons in creating peace in the Middle East.

Frederick had been happily surprised in his arranged marriage to Constance. This time he was not so fortunate. While he and John of Briene waited in Italy, his representatives sailed to the Holy Land to fetch the bride and put the wedding ring on her finger. When she arrived in Brindisi for the wedding ceremony, Frederick was bitterly disappointed. Poor Jolanda of Briene was only thirteen years old, and her new husband was thirty-one. She was not at all pretty and was very short. But because it was a political marriage and not a meeting of hearts in love, Frederick accepted it.

However, he fell in love at first sight with one of the new bride's waiting maids, her cousin Anaïs, who had accompanied Jolanda on the journey. Frederick ran off with Anaïs right after the wedding banquet, which, of course, upset his new bride. Jolanda's father reported the scandal to the Pope, and the story spread throughout Europe as a piece of juicy gossip. Nevertheless, Jolanda later gave birth to Frederick's heir, Conrad, who replaced his half-brother Henry VII as King of the Romans in Germany. Three years after her marriage to Frederick, Jolanda died giving birth to their second child. She was only sixteen.

Frederick waited seven years before marrying again in 1235, at the age of forty-one. It was another political marriage, encouraged and supported by Pope Gregory IX. Frederick was having difficulties with the German princes of the Holy Roman Empire, and the Pope thought that an alliance with the King of England would be helpful. The English king's sister was eligible for marriage and famous for her exquisite beauty. She was twenty-one, twenty years younger than Frederick. An agreement was reached and the marriage arranged. Isabella of England traveled to Germany to meet Frederick and his army, riding at the head of the three thousand knights who accompanied her. Isabella rode through the streets of Cologne richly dressed, taking off her riding hood so that the cheering crowed could admire her beauty. Frederick was pleased with her, yet he treated her poorly, and his young wife must have been unhappy. After the wedding, he had her secluded in the women's quarters of the royal harem, hidden from the eyes of all but her two English waiting maids. Emperor Frederick was so busy dealing with political unrest in Germany that he all but ignored her. Later he moved Isabella to the city of Padua in northern Italy to her own house where he visited her at intervals, especially after she had his child. She bore him four children, two of whom died in infancy. Their son Henry (a second son named Henry) died when he was fifteen. Henry's younger sister Margaret married a German nobleman.

Finally Isabella moved to Palermo in Sicily where she was once visited by her brother, Richard, returning to England from a crusade in the Holy Land. He found her living in quiet seclusion and luxury in the harem. Although she was surrounded by musical instruments and toys for her entertainment, it was obvious that she was not an intimate part of Frederick's life. After six years of marriage, Isabella died in childbirth, only twenty-seven years old.

Bianca Lancia became Frederick's fourth wife and the second woman to win Frederick's heart. Bianca was the daughter of a poor nobleman. Frederick met her for the first time in 1225, a few months after his marriage to Jolanda of Briene. They were both struck by love as if by lightning, and their relationship developed in secret over many years. But being constantly surrounded by numerous people, how secret can an emperor's life be? Because he was already married to Jolanda, he couldn't marry Bianca, but their love grew in spite of his series of political marriages. Bianca remained in the background, a beloved friend who shared Frederick's interests. She was a good listener with an open mind, an accomplished harpist, and a fine singer. She rode horses, accompanying the emperor on falconry hunts. She was well educated and played chess. She was able to look Frederick in the eye and receive his respect. Her quick wit and sense of humor brought a lightness to their relationship. It was not Bianca's modest beauty that was so attractive to Frederick, but rather her intelligence and accomplishments.

As Frederick's wife, Isabella of England had been Queen of Sicily as well as Empress. But when she died, Frederick gave Bianca the lands and possessions that had belonged to Isabella.

Frederick and Bianca had three children. Constance, the eldest, was named after Frederick's mother and first wife. She married Emperor John of Nicea in Constantinople. Violante, their second daughter, married a nobleman and became the Countess of Caserta near Naples. Their son Manfredo was named after the men of the Lancia family, and was noted to be "blond and beautiful." He would reign as King of Sicily after his father. Frederick dedicated his book on falconry to Manfredo. One can imagine Frederick with his arm around Bianca's shoulder and his hand on Manfredo's head as they watched the soaring and swooping flight of the playful swallows from the castle walls at sundown.

"My beloved Bianca."

With a smile on her lips, she turned and said, "Our love has given me so much, but especially this beautiful child."

"Yes," said Frederick, running his fingers through Manfredo's blond curls. "Bianca, how can I please you more?"

"Grant me but one wish, Federico."

"Name it, and it is yours."

"Make our child your legitimate heir."

"To do so I must marry you," he said, looking at her with a serious expression and taking her hand in his.

"I am not a princess," she responded with a hint of humor in her voice.

"But you are my closest friend and have been for many years. Now I will make you my wife." Then he held her close.

"Papa, you are always watching birds. You know so much about them. Perhaps you should write a book about birds and how to hunt with them. You could draw pictures of them, too."

"*Buon idea*, Manfredo, good idea." Frederick smiled at Bianca, who knew he had already been working on his book for many years. "I will call it *De Arte Venandi cum Avibus—The Art of Hunting with Birds*—and you can help me."

"How will we do it, Papa?"

"*By quiet thought and patient attention to details.*"

Chapter 11

Friends and Enemies

As Frederick spoke with Bianca and Manfredo, Piero Della Vigna came running, then stopped short when he saw the three of them. He had been Frederick's trusted friend and counselor for many years. Frederick waved him forward.

"Forgive me, my lord, for interrupting you at this moment, but you will not want to wait to hear the news I bring."

"Out with it, my good man, out with it."

"The Pope … Gregory IX has died."

"My plans to capture the Pope in Rome are no longer necessary. We will not enter Rome with our army. Perhaps the newly-elected Pope will give us peace."

"I fear not, my lord. It is Innocent IV, and he has declared that he will fully carry out Pope Gregory's intention to crush you and your family."

"We must unite the entire Holy Roman Empire and the Kingdom of Italy as a lawful constitutional state."

"The new Pope Innocent maintains your excommunication."

"Excommunication or not, the people live by the laws of the Empire."

"But they follow the teachings of the Church."

"They have more faith in me."

"The Pope incites the northern cities against you and the laws of the Empire."

"Law is the foundation of my government, not force or the compulsion of religion. Mine is a constitutional monarchy based on the laws of the Constitution of Melfi. Law and order, Piero, not submission and slavery. My quarrel is not with the Church but with those who falsely represent her."

Piero was one of the most important judges who helped Frederick to develop the constitution that was written at the emperor's castle at Melfi in Puglia. The laws that Frederick established for his empire were far ahead of their time. For example, he outlawed the use of trial by combat, making it no longer lawful for a case to be judged according to the might of a warrior. While the rest of Europe made the serfs virtual slaves of the land on which they worked, Frederick's laws gave peasants and women the right to inherit land. He formed courts with government-appointed judges who, having full knowledge of the rights of all people, decreased the power of nobles and clergy who up until then had acted as judges over their people. This assured that the laws and judges were impartial to peasant as well as noble, to women as well as men, and to all people regardless of their religion—Moslems, Jews, and Christians.

Freedom of worship was a law for the first time in Europe. Because Frederick had made it possible for women to inherit land, there was no longer a need for a male heir to inherit royal or noble possessions. The law could even make the child of a clergyman legitimate and entitled to a proper upbringing. All children could now be considered legitimate and rightfully able to receive their parents' aid. Those of Frederick's children who were born out of wedlock were supported and either given important positions in their father's government or married into noble families. Frederick wanted his empire ruled by laws that were fair and beneficial to all people regardless of heritage, class, religion, gender, or dwelling place.

Frederick took another step forward. Until this time, silver coins had poorly drawn, cartoon-like images of saints or of the king on them. Frederick brought coins of gold back into use. Gold coins had been in use in ancient Roman times, but had never been minted in Europe. Frederick designed a coin with the imperial eagle on one side and an image of himself as emperor on the other. His gold augustales were wrought with artistic excellence so that his image truly looked like him.

Fig. 11. The Augustalis coin

He had "Imperator Romanus Caesar Augustus" written on them so that all who used them would see his golden image and know who the emperor was.

However, despite all of his advances and innovations and his popularity with his people, the emperor's position was not secure. It became more and more difficult to know which of his subjects and even his friends had been won over by either the Pope's arguments or his gold. Whom could Frederick trust? He lost his son Henry, some of his long-standing allies and closest friends. Attempts were made to assassinate him. The worst blow was the betrayal of his best friend Piero, caught in a plot to overthrow and murder him. To defend himself, Piero faced Frederick and asserted, "But you are excommunicated. How can I continue to serve you?"Frederick shook his head in disbelief, as Piero continued to try to justify himself. "The Pope offers gold and remission of sins to rebels against the state."

"I am sorry, Piero. Take him away," Frederick said to his guards.

Frederick had to imprison his best and longest-lived friend and closest counselor. Whom could he trust now? He had his sons, but could he trust them? He wrote letters to the Pope trying to come to peace, but the Pope would have no peace. His letters to Frederick demanded that he give up everything. The Pope wrote to the emperor's courtiers declaring, "*He must come to me alone, unarmed, and unguarded, as a humble supplicant for mercy. He must abdicate and give up the crown of the empire. He must give all his worldly power to me, the Pope and Vicar of Christ.*"

Frederick wrote back, "*I am crowned by God to rule this world. You rule the souls of men. I rule their lives and deeds through law and justice.*"

The Pope wrote to all the kings and princes of Europe, pronouncing Frederick "*a horned Satan, a hell-hound like Herod, more cruel than Nero, more blasphemous than Belshazzar, more sinful than Lucifer. Because God is with me, my conscience is clear.*"

Frederick responded by stating, "*God is with me because my conscience is clear.*"

Some cities of northern Italy rebelled against Frederick and some remained loyal. The rebellion led to fighting not just against Frederick but also one city against another. Sometimes Frederick was victorious in putting down a rebellion and usually generous in establishing peace. He allowed cities to govern themselves if they obeyed the laws of the empire. Sometimes he could not gain control of a city that fought bravely to defend its independence.

His sons helped Frederick in the battles against the rebels. Central Italy was secured by his sons Richard of Theate and Frederick of Antioch, and northern Italy by his son Enzio of Sardinia and his son-in-law Ezzelino of Romano. Manfredo was his guardian in the south. They had a great victory in the north when they caught the knights of Milan by surprise. As the Milanese came marching down the road singing, Frederick's knights charged out of the forest. The Milanese ran for the small town of Cortenuova nearby. But they were cut down when Frederick sent his mounted Saracen archers after them. Those few who got to the town were able to defend themselves until nightfall when they escaped in the dark.

But Frederick also suffered defeats.

Chapter 12

A Great Loss

While Frederick struggled with the Pope and the northern cities of Italy, a great danger was threatening all of Europe. Genghis Khan led his armies from Mongolia to conquer most of Asia, and his sons led the Mongols to the west. They brutally overran Russia, Poland, and Hungary, and were at the gates of Vienna, Austria. The German princes asked the Pope to call for a crusade of all the kings of Europe to drive the invaders away, but the Pope was too busy with his crusade against Frederick. Frederick's son King Conrad was ruling in Germany, but he was only thirteen years old. So the princes turned to the Emperor Frederick, their overlord, for help. Frederick sent an order for all German knights to defend Europe. In 1241, there was a dreadful battle in which both Germans and Mongols were slaughtered. Then, Genghis Khan died and his armies retreated from Austria to Russia until they could elect a new Khan. Central Europe was saved from defeat at the hands of the barbarian Mongol hordes.

In the meantime, Frederick was also trying to protect the rights of the kings and princes of Europe against the Church's greed for political power. Cardinals, archbishops, and bishops had their own armies and were in control of more and more land which they wanted for their own wealth.

Frederick fought the knights outside the walls of the rebel city of Parma until they retreated into the city and prepared to defend themselves. This was an important battle for Frederick to win. He was determined to hold the enemy forces there until they gave up and surrendered. Frederick camped outside the walls of Parma for a long time. Over six months his encampment grew and became a city itself, which he named Vittoria (Victory). It had walls and towers, canals and bridges, mills and workshops, gardens and orchards, markets and warehouses. Frederick lived there with his sons and counselors and had his treasury brought to him. There he worked on his falconry book while he waited for Parma to give up. It was a long wait. Although he had cut off food supplies to Parma, the people were steadfast and would not surrender. Frederick was often approached by his officers while he observed birds and wrote in his book.

"Shall we attack, my lord?"

"We have surrounded the city for months now. No, we will not attack. We will wait in peace, and perhaps they will peacefully accept the laws of the empire."

"And they will wait for us to leave."

"They know they can govern themselves if they adopt the laws of the empire. We will wait. Do not attack."

"Yes, my lord, as you insist."

"But, you know, as we wait … with spring in the air … on this beautiful day we shall go out to hunt. Prepare the horses and falcons, and tell Manfredo that he must come with us."

"As you wish, my lord."

In Frederick's city of Vittoria, there were spies from Parma. They knew that Enzio was away at that time and reported that Frederick and Manfredo and their company of friends were riding out for a hunt. With Frederick out of the way, the knights of Parma charged out of the city through one gate. When Frederick's troops chased after them, the starving people of Parma, men, women, and children rushed out of another gate and attacked Vittoria. The city was sacked and set on fire. The royal treasury was stolen. Frederick's crown and robes, the imperial seal and scepter, the throne, his library and art treasures—all were seized. The women of his harem were captured and carried off. The mob seized horses and mules and the royal menagerie. They killed or took hundreds of prisoners.

Out on the hunt and unaware of the attack, Frederick heard the alarm bells of Vittoria ringing frantically. He turned his horse and spurred it. He saw the smoke as he galloped back. He and his hunting party charged into the city to fight and defend it, but it was too late.

"My book! Thirty years I have worked on my book. My book! All I wanted was peace to write my book. My book lost...." Vittoria had become his greatest defeat.

At this point Frederick was fifty-four years old. This was not his first defeat nor his last. During the last years of his life he would experience many more defeats as well as victories. In fact, from Vittoria he rode to Cremona, a city in northern Italy that was ever faithful to him. There he rallied his forces and returned within a few days to overtake Parma in the end.

However, Frederick's most tragic losses were his sons. Richard of Theate died and the news struck Frederick deeply. But worse was the capture of Enzio by the knights of Bologna. Enzio and his knights were caught by surprise in open country. He fought bravely right at the front of his men. His horse was shot down, but he jumped onto another. The fight went on all day long, but in the end Enzio was surrounded and taken prisoner. In spite of all the treasures that Frederick was willing to give in exchange for his son, the Bolognese would not release him. They kept him like a bird on display in a golden cage, locked up in a palace of his own in the center of the city. Although he tried to escape, he remained there for twenty-three years, until the end of his life.

Frederick went south to Lucera, the city he built for his Sicilian Saracen subjects. There he was going to prepare his army to march north in the early spring. He planned to conquer Bologna, free Enzio, and then march on to Rome. But he never accomplished his aims. He would meet death first.

Long ago, when he had set out on his crusade to the Holy Land, Frederick had fallen ill. His army was gathered in Puglia and embarking in ships to sail to the Middle East. A plague broke out among the soldiers, who began to die in droves. Frederick sailed on for a couple of days and then got sick himself, so he turned back to recover his health. It was an intestinal illness, probably dysentery. The Pope thought he was making excuses for not going on the crusade and therefore excommunicated him. Frederick regained his health and, after reorganizing his kingdom, he raised an army and headed back to join the crusade. The Pope excommunicated him again, this time for going on crusade when he had already been excommunicated. But Frederick went to the Holy Land and returned with a ten-year truce with the Moslems. He also returned with stomach troubles that would bother him from time to time throughout his life.

Now, as Frederick rode to Lucera, he was very ill, but he did not give it much attention. He went out one day at the end of November to hunt. He had a terrible attack of dysentery that forced him to return to Lucera. The illness was so severe that he was taken instead to the nearer castle of Fiorentino, only a few miles from Lucera. His condition grew worse day by day. He called for his counselors and made out his last will. His favorite son, Manfredo, and his good friend the Archbishop Berardo, who had been loyal to him throughout his life, were with him as he became weaker and weaker. His doctor could do no more for him.

"Help me to sit up, Manfredo," Frederick asked.

"Father, what can I get you?"

"What is it you want?" Berardo asked, as Frederick began to look around the room. He seemed to be searching for something.

"Move out of the way," he said. "What is in that corner? What is the door made of?"

"Father, what is it? What are you looking for? What is troubling you?"

"The door, the door, of what is it made?"

The Archbishop went to the door to the room and replied, "Wood. It is probably oak. Why?"

"The prophecy said an iron door."

"What prophecy, Father?"

Frederick sank back on his pillows and began to tell them of the prophecy. "Long ago, in my youth, a prophet told of my death. He said that I would die *sub flora*, near or under a flower. For that reason, I never went to the city of Florence, *Firenze*. Never! Never would I go to that flower of a city. Now I realize that I am dying in this castle of the little flower, Fiorentino."

"But why did you ask me about the door?" questioned Berardo.

"The prophecy was that I would die *sub flora* near an iron door."

"The door is wooden, Father."

"Search the room. Search the castle. Is there an iron door to be found? Go look!"

They did not want to upset him in his weak condition, so his courtiers went out to search. Manfredo stayed beside his father. Berardo looked around the room and found it. The prophecy was true. Behind the bed above Frederick's head was a tapestry that covered the archway of an iron door that led to an old, unused tower. Manfredo held Frederick in his arms, and said to him, "Father, there is an iron door."

"It is the end. God's will be done," sighed Frederick.

Frederick, still a lay brother of the Cistercian order and wanting to end his life in their simple robes, asked Manfredo and Berardo to help him out of his royal garments and into the white habit of the Cistercian monks. He asked Berardo to hear his last confession so that his sins could be forgiven. After the confession, Berardo gave Frederick that Last Sacrament for the dying. He anointed his eyes, nose, mouth, ears, and hands with holy oil while he recited the prayers. Frederick received the sacrament in peace. Other friends and counselors joined Manfredo and Berardo to be with Frederick as his life came to an end. It was December 13th, 1250. His fifty-sixth birthday was thirteen days away.

Frederick faced his death fearlessly and steadfastly, as he had faced all the challenges in his life.

Frederick had asked to have a very simple, modest funeral, but his children, friends, and subjects would not honor his request. They saw him as a great man and wished him to be mourned and buried in splendor and ceremony. His body was dressed in royal robes and covered with a cloth of crimson velvet. It was placed on a bier and carried by his Saracen bodyguards with more of them surrounding it and following on foot. They wept openly as they carried the body. There were six companies of mounted knights leading the way, followed by the Saracens. They made their way through the region of Puglia, where people lined the roads for miles to say a farewell prayer for their king and emperor. As the procession approached the cities along their way, governors, barons, and noble men and women came out dressed in black to accompany Frederick's body through his realms. The procession paused in Bitonto, where his body was brought into the cathedral. A seemingly endless stream of people filed in to pray over Frederick. Heralds with trumpets blew a fanfare and announced, "The Emperor Frederick is dead. Long live the Emperor Conrad!" Frederick's son Conrad would later be elected emperor in his place.

From the cathedral in Bitonto the procession continued through Puglia to Frederick's castle in Gioia del Colle, where Bianca Lancia had lived for many years, then on to the city of Taranto. There the bier was placed on a ship that set sail for Sicily. When the ship came to port in Palermo, the people of the city were waiting at the docks in the harbor. A wailing arose from the crowd as the procession made its way through the streets to the cathedral. People dropped to their knees as the bier passed them. The bier was carried through the bright searing light and the brilliant blue of the Sicilian day into the somber shadows of the house of God.

Frederick's body was then dressed in a garment of linen that had Arabic embroidery of gold thread on the sleeves and a crusader's cross sewn over his heart. A red silk robe and a mantle embroidered with the imperial eagles were clasped on with a jeweled brooch. His silken boots were embroidered with images of deer and clasped with golden spurs. On his head was placed a Byzantine crown covered with jewels, and on his finger a golden ring with a large emerald. A purse was on his belt. His sword, sheathed with Saracen craftsmanship, was placed at his side along with a scepter and an imperial orb filled with earth.

Dressed in these rich vestments, the body was placed in a sarcophagus of a purple rock called porphyry. To this day the sarcophagus rests on a stand shaped like lions, and it is roofed with a canopy on columns, all of the same purple porphyry. Alongside his tomb is a similar one in which his first wife, Constance of Aragon, is buried, and near these, behind a wrought-iron railing, are the tombs of his parents, Henry VI and Constance d'Hautville, and his grandfather Roger II. There, entombed in the imperial purple stone of the ancient Roman emperors, lie the greatest rulers of Sicily. Even today one can always find a bouquet of fresh red roses standing before Frederick's tomb. Visitors still come after more than seven hundred years to place them in his honor and remember *Il Stupor Mundi*, "The Wonder of the World."

Chapter 13

The Vendetta

When news of Frederick's death reached Pope Innocent IV, he declared, "*Let us rejoice and be glad,*" to which the congregation surrounding him responded with, "*Down to Hell he went.*" But the Pope's feud with the emperor did not end with Frederick's death. Frederick had many children both in and out of wedlock, and the Hohenstaufens were a large family. Many of Frederick's descendants held important and powerful positions in southern Italy and in the Holy Roman Empire. The Pope was determined to keep these two realms separate for good and to protect the borders of his Papal States in central Italy. His goal could only be achieved if he eliminated Frederick's family. He needed to find political allies, noblemen who would overthrow the Hohenstaufens and be loyal to the Papacy.

The crusade was now turned against Conrad, Frederick's son, who ruled in Germany. Conrad left his young son Conradin on the throne in Germany and went to Italy to restore order. At the time of Frederick's death, his forces were more successful in subduing the rebellious cities of northern Italy. Conrad went to consolidate the north, while his half-brother Manfredo ruled the south of Italy as his regent. But Conrad died four years after his father.

With Conrad out of the way, the Pope went into action. He sent the nobleman William of Orange from Holland to win the support of the German princes in a bid to take the place of young Conradin. At the same time he searched for someone to overthrow Manfredo. He appealed to the English, but they were not interested in Sicily. The Pope, still living safely in Lyon, France, to keep away from the Hohenstaufens, turned to the King of France, but Louis IX continued to remain neutral in the conflict between the Popes and Frederick.

But King Louis' brother, Charles of Anjou, was a candidate for leader of the crusade against the Hohenstaufens. He had his own army and money but received additional funds from the Church as well as the support of the Pope's army. Charles accepted the task and was crowned king of southern Italy. He was joined by knights from France, Provence, Italy, Germany, England, and Spain, all of whom hoped to receive land and titles in southern Italy from Charles, as well as forgiveness for their sins from the Pope.

The year was 1266. It had taken sixteen years for the Pope to find a leader for his crusade against Frederick's dynasty. During that time Manfredo ruled as his father had, maintaining a cultured court and a government based on justice. But once Charles of Anjou was given the Pope's blessing, he conquered southern Italy in two weeks and took control of the kingdom. It was a formidable opponent that Manfredo faced. He engaged them in battle and lost. Courageously refusing to flee from the battlefield, Manfredo was cut down. He died leading his men in the fight.

The defeated southern kingdom appealed to young King Conradin, Frederick's grandson on the throne in Germany. He was only fourteen years old when he led his army to help the Hohenstaufen cause against the invading Charles of Anjou. When Frederick was in his teens, he had gone north to Germany to take his grandfather's place on the throne. Now his grandson was coming south to take Frederick's place. As Frederick's youth and innocence had enchanted the people and drawn them to him, so did Conradin's. He was the new hope for Italy, and the cities of the south and their barons rallied around him. The King of Tunis in north Africa, who was a vassal of Frederick's, sent an army to Sicily to help Conradin. Prince Henry of Castile, Spain, who had come to Italy with Charles, did not receive the reward that he had expected. So he turned on Charles and became one of Conradin's most important generals.

As Conradin marched south, Charles went east to attack the stronghold of Frederick's Saracens in Lucera, Puglia. Then he turned to face the young king and his powerful army. The battle was tremendous, with heavy losses on both sides. At first Conradin was winning, but Charles' troops regrouped and finally defeated the courageous but inexperienced Conradin and his troops. Conradin escaped with some of his friends, but they were captured soon after and taken to the city of Naples to stand trial. To the horror of the people, the young king and his friends were condemned to be publicly executed. The heroic Conradin, at age sixteen, was beheaded on the block in the great piazza.

When the news of Conradin's execution reached his uncle Enzio, imprisoned in his palace in Bologna, he was shocked and distraught, and quickly determined to escape. He wanted to take up the fight against Charles of Anjou and save his family's right to sovereignty. But how could he get out of Bologna? He hid himself in a big, empty wine barrel among many others that were to be taken out to the countryside to be refilled in the vineyards. The timing was delicate. How long would it be until his captors realized that he was missing? He had to leave the barrel's bung hole open to provide him with sufficient air to breathe while he waited for the barrel to be loaded on a cart. His guards soon noticed his absence and a cry went up as they began to search the palace and the city streets. The cart started on its way but it was stopped at the city gate. As the guards examined the cart full of barrels, one noticed a lock of hair sticking out of a bung hole. Enzio was caught again and returned to his palace with an escort of guards. Disappointed by his failure, he became more and more depressed. He died in his palatial prison two years later.

Manfredo's second wife, Helena, and their children were captured in Puglia. She was separated from her young children, and they were put in different prisons. The children, who were named after their grandparents and uncles, Frederick, Henry, and Enzio, and their sister, Beatrice, were held in Castel del Monte. Helena was distraught and worried about them, not knowing where they were or what had happened to them. She soon became sick with the grief and loss, and died not knowing the fate of her children. After ten years in prison Beatrice was released because she was a girl and not considered a threat by Charles of Anjou. On the other hand, the boys were considered very dangerous indeed. Imprisoned in Castel del Monte for thirty years, they grew from infants to boys to men. Enzio died there. Frederick and Henry did finally leave the castle, but they were not given freedom. Instead, they were moved to the Castel dell' Ovo (the Egg) on a rock in the sea outside the city of Naples. On the way there, Frederick, having a zest for life and as spirited as his grandfather, made his escape. He got away successfully, but he could not find anyone in Europe to help him recover his crown. He traveled all over, from Italy to Germany to England to Spain, and was last known to be in Egypt, but his fate seems to have disappeared in the desert sands. His brother Henry languished in the dungeon of Castel dell' Ovo. He grew steadily weaker, eventually went blind, and died. He was buried, like an animal, in an unmarked grave.

One of Frederick's grandsons did escape when the forces of the Pope and Charles of Anjou tried to eliminate the Hohenstaufen family: Conrad of Antioch, the son of Frederick of Antioch and Margaret. Frederick of Antioch died before Manfredo and Conradin, but Margaret saved their son. She held two prisoners in her castle, two members of an important family who was loyal to Charles of Anjou. When her son was captured, she exchanged her two prisoners for his freedom. To this day there is a town about twenty-five miles from Rome called Anticoli Corrado. The villagers whose last name is Corrado, the Italian version of Conrad, claim they are descendants of Conrad of Antioch, the grandson of Frederick II.

Although we do not know who their mothers were, Frederick had at least five other known daughters. They were not his legitimate heirs, but he recognized them as his descendants, and married them all to noblemen. His granddaughter Constance, the daughter of Manfredo and his first wife, Beatrice of Savoy, played an important role in the future of Sicily. Constance was named after her grandmother, Constance of Aragon, Frederick's first wife. Young Constance married Peter of Aragon, and they lived in Spain.

In Sicily, the French rulers under Charles of Anjou were oppressive. In Palermo, on the Tuesday after Easter in 1282, the bells of the cathedral rang at vespers, the late afternoon call to prayer service. A group of women walked to the church together, chatting as they strolled along. Their husbands, boyfriends, and relatives also walked together but lagged behind them. Some French soldiers saw the women, found them very attractive, and followed, trying to get their attention and to flirt with them. When the women ignored the soldiers, they became more forward and then aggressive. When the women continued to go their way, telling the soldiers to mind their own business and leave them alone, a Frenchman grabbed one of the women. She screamed and struck the soldier. His friends pulled him away. The scuffle grew more rough and heated, and louder. Their husbands and boyfriends heard the women's cries and ran to the rescue. It was a great insult for a French soldier to touch a Sicilian woman. The men began to fight in earnest and a crowd began to gather. A knife was drawn and a soldier fell under its stroke. Someone yelled out, "Death to the French!" The Sicilians began to attack and kill any and all the French they could find. The rebellion of the oppressed people flared up in the faces of their oppressors and spread from the cathedral throughout the city. No Frenchman was safe. They were surprised, outnumbered, and overwhelmed.

From Palermo the rebellion, known as the Sicilian Vespers, spread throughout the island. When the news of it reached Charles of Anjou, he turned his army in southern Italy and marched toward Sicily. The Sicilians turned to Peter of Aragon for help because he was married to a Hohenstaufen, Constance, to whom they were still devoted. He came to their rescue. Just as Charles landed on the eastern shore of Sicily, Peter arrived on the western shore of the island. Peter's Spaniards and the Sicilians drove the French out. Peter continued to lead his army to southern Italy in hope of regaining Frederick's kingdom.

The French held out and kept southern Italy, but Peter of Aragon and Constance became king and queen of Sicily. The Spanish would rule Sicily and eventually southern Italy for more than five hundred years. But none of these kings would rise to the greatness of Frederick, the "Wonder of the World." Those glorious days were over.

Chapter 14

The Future

Unfortunately, it is often the victors who write the history that comes down to us, and much of what we know about Frederick has been handed down by his enemies. Because Frederick's realms, power, and influence were lost to his family after his death, his enemies left their portrayals of him as the Antichrist, the Devil himself. The great poet Dante Alighieri was born in Florence only fifteen years after Frederick died, but Frederick's reputation was already ruined. In his masterpiece, *The Divine Comedy*, Dante described heaven, purgatory, and hell, placing Frederick in hell for his sins.

Although Pope Innocent IV said, "Let us rejoice and be glad," when he heard of Frederick's death, others felt differently. Michael Scotus, Frederick's court philosopher and a wise man in many subjects, said, with regard to the emperor's death, "*The sun of the world has set, which illuminated all people. The sun of justice has set, and so has the love of peace.*" Berardo, the Archbishop of Palermo, who, of all men, perhaps knew Frederick longest, said, "*If uprightness, intelligence, valor, and nobility could overcome death, Frederick would not be dead.*"

Pope Innocent IV considered Frederick unworthy to be a Christian ruler. He believed that the Moslems were the evil enemies of Christianity, and that it was sacrilege for them to hold the Holy

Land, while Frederick recognized the Holy Land as a place sacred to Christians, Jews, and Moslems alike. The Sultan of Egypt, al-Kamil, was a Moslem leader who met with Frederick to negotiate a truce meant to create a peace among the Moslems, Christians and Jews in the Middle East. He described Frederick differently from the Pope: "*We spoke of questions of mathematics, logic, statecraft, and religion. He spoke my language well. He was strong, and had a well-knit body, keen eye, quick mind and tongue, and universal interests.*"

As al-Kamil pointed out, Frederick was a man of universal interests and a seeker after truth. He had questions about everything under the sun, including questions about faith and religion and life after death. After Frederick's death, one of the high officials of the Pope's court, Cardinal Salimbene, tried to make a statement that was critical of Frederick, but seemed unable to resist praising him: "*As to faith in God, he had none. He was an ingenious, cunning man, greedy, wanton, malicious, bad tempered. But at times he was a worthy man, when he wished to reveal his good and courtly qualities, consoling, witty, delightful, hard working. He could read, write, and sing, he could compose music and songs. He was a handsome man, well built of medium stature. I have seen him, and at one time esteemed him highly. ... Also he could speak many languages. In short, if he had been a good Catholic, loved God and His Church, and his own soul, he would have had few equals among the emperors of the world.*"

Frederick was a dynamic individual, a deep thinker, a lover of life who lived with gusto. He had an indomitable will. He was a scientist, interested in all natural phenomena, who wrote a comprehensive treatise on falconry that is still read today. He was an artist, practicing architecture, poetry, drawing, and music. He was not a religious man, yet he was keenly interested in the religions of others as well as his own people. Frederick may have been the only emperor in history whose interest in the world and its people was so broad and deep. He consulted theologians, scientists, and artists the world over, but he would also stop in his travels to ask a shepherd about his breed of sheep or a farmer how he grew his peas.

Although he cultivated a life of the mind throughout his life, Frederick was a ruler, a leader of people and a man of action. He was born a king and elected an emperor. He took his responsibilities seriously and made great strides in advancing the culture and prosperity of his people. A man with so much character and intellectual strength as well as political power was threatening to many people. Some admired him. Some hated him. He was strong, and so he drew strong reactions from others, both positive and negative.

It was Frederick's destiny to be a great man. He led the way into the future. In time the sciences he advanced would develop in an age when explorers discovered the richness of the earth's lands and seas and the vastness of space through geography, astronomy, and physics. The medical school that Frederick founded would continue to support the evolution of chemistry, biology, physiology, and further studies in mathematics. His laws and constitutions initiated a just and idealistic government that would develop in a later age, the Age of the Renaissance. His struggle with the Church to achieve the separation of government and religion, among many other changes, would come to fulfillment in the future Reformation. Frederick II of Hohenstaufen was a worthy, if not universally recognized, hero in his time, and his values would stand us in good stead in our own time.

But for now, let us leave Frederick where we first encountered him, standing on the walls of his palace in Palermo. ...

"But, Piero, I can't take time for this letter now. I have a bird on wing, a beauty."

"Yes, Federico, but it is important. You must protect your relationship with the King of France."

"Yes, yes," said Federico with a frown. "He has not answered my letter asking for his understanding and support of my position in regard to that God-awful Pope. God forgive me, but he is awful, and now he has retreated to France."

"But, Federico ..."

"Yes, yes, yes, send him another letter, for God's ... for goodness sake, and refer to my last letter. Of course, thank him for the greetings he sent for my birthday. And send a gift along."

"It's a fine gesture, Your Majesty, my dear Federico," said Piero smiling.

With an answering smile, Federico said, "But, Piero, look at this bird fly! It is a grillaio given to me by Fuccio, the architect from Firenze, the one who is designing my cathedral in Altamura. He says that the sky over the city of Altamura is darkened every sunset by the flight of these little beauties as they go out to hunt for their supper. And this particular one that he sent was trained to ..."

"Yes, Your Majesty," said Piero, watching how animated Frederick became as he talked about his beloved birds.

"Oh, but you must see how well she returns without using a lure. A mere whistle will bring her back to me. And I know that I have work to do, but you must take time to enjoy yourself, Piero."

"I will enjoy your company at dinner this evening, Federico. You can tell me more about this grillaio from Altamura."

"In the dialect of Altamura, they call the grillaio U' tressciunghele. What a tongue-twister!" said Frederick with delight.

"Your Majesty?" said Piero with a bow.

"Yes, yes, go, Piero, I will tell you more later," said Frederick, turning to watch the soaring grillaio from the castle wall. He gave a sharp whistle to call the bird back to him. It gave a quick dip of its wing, then turned to continue on its own course. Frederick whistled again, but the soaring bird did not respond. Frederick picked up the lure on a string and began to swing it around to attract the bird's attention. He saw its wings dip again for a moment and its head turn, but Frederick could see that it was not going to turn back to him, though he thought he had trained it well. "Ah," he said aloud to himself, "sometimes we send things out into the world, our thoughts, our words, our deeds, or even a strong-willed bird, like this one, and we don't really know what they will do, what will become of them. Only the future will tell ... and we may not be here to see it. We just have to let them go. *Vola, cara mia.* Fly. Fly, my lovely."

Finito

Notes

Page 16 and following — Much of the dialog of Archbishop Berardo and the various Popes is historically documented, taken from records of the actual words spoken or from letters written at that time. The appropriate quotes have been italicized to make this clear.

Page 34 — The crown that Frederick put in Queen Constance's tomb can be seen today in the treasury of the cathedral in Palermo. It is unusual for a crown and very beautiful.

Pages 20 and 43 — The Albigensian Crusade was declared by Pope Innocent III in 1208 and ended in 1244. It was a war waged by the Pope and the King of France against the Cathar Christians of Provence, southern France. The Cathars criticized the Roman Catholic Church, like many others at that time, including Francis of Assisi. During those years, Frederick was between 14 and 50 years old.

Page 61 — This chapter is based on a popular legend from southern Italy, not known to be a historical fact through documentation. A plaque found recently in Frederick's castle in Bari agrees with the main points of the traditional story. Francis of Assisi was 12 years old when Frederick was born. Pope Gregory IX accepted Francis as the leader of a new monastic order rather than as a heretic who, like the Cathars, also objected to the Catholic Church's abundant wealth. Thus, the Pope was able to use the Franciscans in his mission against Frederick.

Pages 10, 19, 24 91–92, 94–96 and 99

Hohenstaufen is Frederick's father's family name and d'Hauteville is his mother's family name.

Further Reading

For teachers –

The Amazing Frederic by Gertrude Slaughter, Macmillan, 1937 (my favorite)

For scholars –

Frederick II of Hohenstaufen, A Life by Georgina Masson, Secker & Warburg, 1957

Frederick II, A Medieval Emperor by David Abulafia, Oxford University Press, 1988

The Art of Falconry by Frederick Roger Hohenstaufen, Stanford University Press, 1961

Novels –

The Falcon of Palermo by Maria R. Bordihn, Atlantic Monthly, 2005.

Antichrist by Cecelia Holland, Atheneum, 1970

For children – (about Frederick's childhood)

The King's Road by Cecelia Holland, Atheneum, 1970

Website – www.stupormundi.it.